SOLVED!

The "Mysterious" Disappearance
of Jim Thompson,
the Legendary Thai Silk King

SOLVED!

The "Mysterious" Disappearance
of Jim Thompson,
the Legendary Thai Silk King

Edward Roy De Souza

Copyright © 2004 by Edward Roy De Souza

All rights reserved. No part of this book may be used or reproduced in any manner whatsoever without written permission of the author.

Printed in the United States of America.

ISBN: 1-932205-89-6
Library of Congress Control Number: 2004101795

Word Association Publishers
205 5th Avenue
Tarentum, PA 15084
www.wordassociation.com

To:

Andrew Trevatt
Panadura Chandra Sena
Jayant Kumar Dey
Dr Desmond Oon Seng Wah

Acknowledgements

I would like to thank the following for being a tremendous source of encouragement to me: Amin Bin Suratin, Andrew T.H. Lim, Ang Boon Tien, Anthony A.S. Lewis, Barry White, Belly Anak Wah, Bernard Teo Tiat How, Brant LeBlanc, C.T. Lim, Chang Kee Tong, Christopher K.Y. Liew, Danny Teo, David Wong Kim, Dublin Anak Ijali, Eddie Lee Choon Guan, Estie Lim, Foong Chow Weng, Goh Lip Siah, Goh Tang Meng, Gordon Parnaby, Hermann Tay, Herold Thng, Htayy Win, Ibrahim Bin Mat, Irene Toh Lay Kuan, Ishak Mohamed Ali, James Koh, James Youngblood, Jeffrey Edwards, Johnny Liso, Johnny Ong Koon Tin, Joseph Carp, Joseph Duggar, K. Sashidaran, Kenneth Chan Pong Heng, Kenneth Miller, Keramjit Singh, Kevin Banks, Koh Yeow Chiang, Komati Hari Prasad, Lee Kermit Kelling, Lim Choon Teck, Lloyd Pereira, Malcolm Gallistan, Michael Foster, Michael Hawkins, Michael Lee Ballard, Noorisham Abdullah, Philip Ong Meng Tiong, Ray Chan Weng Yong, Richard Teo Ah Fong, Robert Conceicao, Roger Dennerly, Rony Hendarmin, Rony Lee Nam San, S. Murali, S. Kathiravan, S. Sathiyannesan, Sebastian Lee, Seta Anak Padong, Sia Kwang Yiau, Sujoy Dey, Thomas Thiru, Toh Poh Soon, Ulrich Kuhlmann, Vincent Lee See Chai, Y.K. Choo, Yeo Ek Seng, Yeo Khim Hwa, Yong Per Muh and Zayani Suparman.

Illustrations Credits
Pak Ah Bee

Contents

Abbreviations viii
Prologue.. ix
Chapter One 1
Chapter Two 3
Chapter Three 5
Chapter Four 9
Chapter Five 13
Chapter Six 17
Chapter Seven 21
Chapter Eight 25
Chapter Nine 29
Chapter Ten 31
Chapter Eleven 37
Chapter Twelve 45
Chapter Thirteen 47
Chapter Fourteen 55
Chapter Fifteen 57
Chapter Sixteen 59
Postscript 65
Map of Northwest Malaysia 68
Epilogue 69
Glossary 77
Index 79

Center Spread Illustrations (in alphabetical order):
Che Fatimah binte Mohamed Yeh, Constance (Connie) Mangskau, Dadi Balsara, Dennis Horgan, Edwin Black, Helen Ling, Jim Thompson, Peter Hurkos, Pridi Panomyong, Richard Noone, T.G. Ling and Thong Weng.

Center Spread Gate (front)
Map of The Cameron Highlands

Center Spread Gate (rear)
Map of Kamunting Precinct

Abbreviations

a.k.a.	also known as.
ACP	Assistant Commissioner of Police.
ASP	Assistant Superintendent of Police.
CIA	Central Intelligence Agency.
Del.	Delaware (USA).
Dr	Doctor.
Gen	General.
Interpol	International Criminal Police Organization.
km	kilometer.
Lt	lieutenant.
Ltd	Limited.
m	meter(s).
N.Y.	New York (USA).
No.	Number.
OMF	Overseas Mission Fellowship.
OSS	Office of Strategic Services.
Ph.D	Doctor of Philosophy.
Pte	Private.
RM	Ringgit Malaysia (Malaysian currency).
RMAF	Royal Malaysian Air Force.
SEATO	Southeast Asia Treaty Organization.
US	United States.
USA	United States of America.
via	by way of.
viz.	namely.

Prologue

The numbered paths in this book are not to scale: they are only meant to serve as a guide as to where they could be found.

If you are planning to go for a walk, do check with someone reliable as to whether the trail you intend to take is indeed a suitable one. As far as possible, do not start a walk late in the afternoon. Depending on its distance, some paths can take as long as three to five hours to cover.

If, by chance, you lose your way, do not continue on from wherever you are. It would be wise to stop and return to where you first came from.

Whether you are going for a long walk or a short one, do not burden yourself with a whole load of items. A compass, a reliable map, a whistle, a lighter, a filled water bottle, a torch, a raincoat, a jack knife and some snacks are some of the things you should bring along with you.

Whatever it is, do not go for a walk all by yourself. If you do so, do keep someone informed of the track you intend to take and the time you are expected to be back.

Chapter One

The hunt was for one man. He came to the Cameron Highlands for a short holiday. Two days later, he disappeared.

When he left the villa, no one was supposedly kept informed. His friends took it that he had gone for a mid-afternoon stroll. They were quite sure he would return by six. When he failed to do so, they began to sense that something was amiss. To ascertain as to what was possibly wrong, one of them got into his car and made his way to a nearby club. He had high hopes of meeting him along the way. But his drive in that direction drew a blank. For a while, he was in two minds as to what he should do next. A little later, he felt that it would be wise of him to give a call to his rental agents to see if they could be of any help. Just after he had done so, he went ahead and kept in touch with the police. He was told that word of his friend's disappearance would be made known to the settlements in the area. It was also revealed to him that if his friend failed to show up, an inquiry would be conducted the next morning.

On his return from the station, he came into contact with two visitors: one was his rental agent; the other was a major from the British army. After a short discussion, they left the premises and made their way to a nearby hill. The place was given a brief inspection but their quest to spot him did not amount to much. Puzzled as to where he could possibly be found, the two returned to the detached house to see if they could gather more clues with regard to his likely whereabouts. A little after midnight, they left the cottage and made another attempt to find for him at an entirely different location. But their second endeavor, like the first, produced no results.

At sunrise, about five policemen showed up at the bungalow. After

Solved!

taking down his particulars, they left the scene. Later that day, the police, with the help of thirty aborigines, carried out a search of their own. Their review was relatively thorough but there was just no trace of him. Before noon, word of his mysterious disappearance began to spread like wild fire. By now, more than a hundred people were looking high and low for him. The area was given a once-over but their hunt proved to be a disappointment.

The next day, a Tuesday, saw the biggest investigation mounted in Malaysian history. Tanah Rata, in fact, the whole of the Cameron Highlands, was agog with excitement. At ground level, troops crisscrossed the jungle. Above, a few helicopters were seen snooping over the treetops. In all, more than five hundred people were on the look out for one man. It included no less than three hundred officers and men from Perak's police field force, scores of tourists, residents, aborigines, American school students and British servicemen resting at the resort.

Overall, the probe was well organized. It was initially confined to within an eight-kilometer radius of "Moonlight" bungalow. The areas covered were the Robinson waterfall, the golf course, the recreation ground, and the surrounding hills and ravines. Till late in the evening, no one was able to detect him. At the end of the day, the police came to two conclusions: Jim could either be trapped or he could have accidentally injured himself. But they were in no way discouraged, being quite certain that Jim would be found. At the back of their minds they thought he would somehow or other be able to find his way back. As far as they were concerned, it was more a question of time than anything else.

Chapter Two

James (Jim) Harrison Wilson Thompson was born on March 21, 1906 in Greenville, Delaware, USA. He spent his early years of education at St Paul's boarding school. He later went on to enroll at Princeton. Postgraduate studies followed at the University of Pennsylvania's School of Architecture but he failed to get his degree at this institution due to his weakness in calculus.

In 1931, he settled for a career which involved the designing of homes for the East Coast rich. In the initial stages of his employment, he found his assignments to be both rewarding and satisfying. After a while, the glamour of being an architect lost its attention for him. In 1941, he gave up his job and joined the Delaware National Guard. Five years later, he was commissioned as a lieutenant. Just before the outbreak of the Second World War, he was transferred to a military outpost in Fort Monroe, Virginia. It was here that he got to know two persons, both of whom were to have a dramatic impact on his life.

The first was Patricia (Pat) Thraves; the other, Edwin Black. The former was a voluptuous model. He was simply carried away by her beauty and alluring mannerisms. After a whirlwind courtship, he went ahead and married her.

The latter was a fresh graduate from the military college of West Point. He encouraged Jim to come with him to Washington to join a relatively new outfit which was known as the Office of Strategic Services (OSS). Without any hesitation, Jim did so.

He found his new job at the OSS – the frontrunner of the Central Intelligence Agency – to be a lot more interesting. As a spy, he was given a free hand to put his raw talents and creativity to good use. But there was a drawback to his career: it required of him to be away from home at short notice. However, this did not in the least bother him.

Solved!

His first call of duty was with the French resistance forces in North Africa. A little later, arrangements were made for him to be sent to Europe. At the height of the Second World War, large areas of the Continent were under the control of the Germans. Jim, who was now approaching forty, was assigned the task of destroying their communication centers. It was not an easy assignment but he managed to perform his duties to expectation. Within a span of six months, he was promoted twice – first to the rank of captain, then to the position of major.

While he was still engaged in Europe, his wife began to turn her back on him. He came to realize that there was now a growing coldness between the two of them. To get his mind off her, he requested for a posting in East Asia. Eight weeks later his application was accepted.

His initial posting was in the volatile China-Burma-India war zone. While based there, he was upgraded to the rank of lieutenant colonel. His next station was in Ceylon (now Sri Lanka) where he was put in charge of the pro-Allied *Seri Thai* or Free Thai Movement. The guerrillas under him were trained to carry out clandestine activities against their occupiers. For months they were taught how to live off the land. Their training was indeed rigorous and it received the full support of Pridi Panomyong and Seni Pramoj. Pridi, a brilliant French-trained lawyer, was at that time serving as regent to Ananda Mahidol, the then king of Thailand. Seni, on the other hand, was a Thai politician who was based in the United States. Both Pridi and Seni were of one mind – they were ever determined to see the Japanese out of their country. In 1945, their long-time wish was fulfilled. In late July that year, arrangements were made to help liberate the country. But two developments held back the plans of the Free Thai Movement: on August 6, the atomic bomb fell on Hiroshima; three days later, Nagasaki was hit. For the next few days, Jim and the members of his group were instructed to stay put at wherever they were operating. Six days later, they left their base and got themselves ready to penetrate into central Thailand. Their role was to get the locals to form some sort of a resistance against the Japanese. Their plan, however, did not come to pass. While they were on their way to Thailand, they were informed that the war in Asia had come to an abrupt end. The bombings of Hiroshima and Nagasaki proved to be a success – tens of thousands perished from the impact. Fearing further destruction to their other cities, the Japanese opted to surrender. This was followed by the immediate withdrawal of their troops from the area. With their departure, peace was once again restored to the Asia-Pacific region.

Chapter Three

After the war, Jim flew in to Bangkok. He realized that the city was a lot different from what he had made it out to be. On land, the people moved around in a pedicab or *samloh*. Off land, the traffic commuted via the town's canals or *klongs*. On the whole, he noticed that the Thais were not only proud of their culture; by nature, they were charming as well.

"Thailand," he observed, "reminds me of the Delaware of my boyhood. When I was young, I always had the feeling that the world around me was full of surprises. I consider Thailand to be one such place."

To a considerable extent, it was so. While he was in Thailand, he was assigned to the US embassy to serve as its military attaché. During his free time, he took the occasion to explore the remote areas of the country. His upland visits sometimes took him to as far as the borders of Laos and Myanmar.

While he was still in service, he did entertain the thought of wanting to make Thailand his new home. Along the way, he got to know quite a number of people, some of whom held high-ranking positions. Later it came to his knowledge that the famed Oriental Hotel in Bangkok was up for sale. He seized upon the chance and bought about twenty-five per cent of its shares. The hotel – which was previously used by the Japanese High Command – was in a bad shape when he and his other partners took over the running of the place. But he was in no way discouraged by its poor condition. In short, he was positive it had the potential of being what it once used to be.

After spending about a year in the country, it now dawned on him that he had to decide as to whether he wanted to go on being in the army or to seek a discharge from it. Of the two, he chose the latter. While he

Solved!

was back home, he met up with his wife and tried to bring their nine-month-old marriage into line. During the attempted reconciliation, he tried to persuade her to return with him to Thailand. Suffice it to say, she was not in favor of it. Their parting of ways had a great effect on him. He returned to Thailand a broken man. For the next few months, he was optimistic that his hotel venture would take off. It never did. While working on its improvement, he had several differences with some of his associates and this resulted in him giving up his shares altogether.

While casting about for a suitable profession, he found himself spending more time exploring the outskirts of the country. On some of his highland visits, he came across the presence of looms in quite a number of homes. On inquiring about their significance, he was told that they were for the weaving of silk. When handed a piece of the hand-finished cloth, he realized it was quite unlike any other that he had laid his hands on. From what he knew, he had struck a treasure. His father had been in the textile business for years. While assisting him, he developed a fine eye for judging various types of materials – one of them was silk. In all his travels, he had never seen or felt anything more exquisite than Thai silk. But what came as a surprise to him was this: in spite of its richness, Thai silk was relatively unknown to the outside world; it was not even sold on a large scale in Thailand itself. Each family wove just enough for their own use. After giving it serious thought, he was convinced it had commercial possibilities. But three aspects of its production had to undergo a change: one, the fabric had to be woven into saleable lengths; two, the vegetable dyes in use had to be replaced with aniline; lastly, a fresh set of designs had to be incorporated into the finished product to help create an interest in the material.

Initially, he had a hard time putting his ideas across. His inability to communicate with the weavers was one drawback; their resistance to change was another. But he remained tenacious, going on to search the country's weavers. He finally came across a group of weavers from Bangkrua who was more than prepared to give his ideas a try.

In 1947, he bought about US$100 worth of their merchandise and made his way to New York. While he was there, he got to know Edna Woolman Chase, then the editor of *Vogue*. She was indeed impressed with the silk he had brought along with him. Later, without his even knowing it, she engaged Valentina, a New York designer, to fashion a dress out of his material. A couple of weeks later, she saw to it that the details of the outfit were featured in her monthly publication. This marked the fashionable revival of Thai silk which had all but vanished due to cheaper imports from Europe and Japan.

Jim was particularly excited that silk was gradually becoming a hit among the fashion-conscious. A year later, he returned to Thailand with the clear intention of going into the business. While moving around, he came across a run-down shop which sold Thai silk. For a while, he toyed with the idea that he could improve on the quality of the material. But he realized he was unable to do so immediately because of a shortage of funds. That same year, however, a chance came his way. He met George Barrie, an old-time friend from Santa Monica, California. He brought George to the Chinese silk shop. George was amazed at what he saw. At first sight, he knew Thai silk had the potential of being a marketable item. Towards the end of 1948, George partnered Jim to form the Thai Silk Company. It was capitalized at US$25,000. They each bought eighteen per cent of its shares. The remaining sixty-four per cent were sold to both Thai and foreign investors.

The real breakthrough came in 1951 when renowned designer Irene Shareff made use of Thai silk fabrics for the Roger's and Hammerstein musical, *The King and I*. From then on, the company prospered. Three years after its founding, the shareholders of the company enjoyed a one hundred per cent dividend. Their staff too were rewarded with three months' wages plus twenty per cent of the company's profits.

Jim's discovery of the industry raised many an eyebrow. Despite being a new comer, over time, the company outgrew its beginnings. During its infancy, the company had to compete with about eighty establishments selling Thai silk. By the mid-1960s, the figure rose to one hundred and twenty-five. On the whole, there was no big secret to the company's style of doing business; in essence, it operated much like a cooperative. Several weaving groups worked for the organization. People who owned from four to a hundred looms produced the silk. The firm provided them with dyes, designs and financial support. On their part, they had to adhere to the requirements of the company.

Jim used to visit the different looms every morning. During his daily rounds he made it a point to check on the previous day's work. His formula for success was not as complex as what one would make it out to be. In brief, it hinged on two factors.

"In the first instance," he said, "we run a dependable operation. Whenever we come up with a pattern or color that sells well, we make

Solved!

sure we stick to its exact formula. That way, our customers can rest assured that when they re-order, they will get a consistent product."

"Equally important," he mentioned, "is that the cottage industry in this part of the world is more significant than what most people realize. Most of the weavers in this area either don't care or don't need to know who are buying their products. But it is necessary for us to know what our customers' tastes and requirements are."

Jim added, "The Thai silk-weavers technique is hundreds of years old. Every child learns how to weave but each family weaves only enough for its own needs. Their styles and colors are not suitable for foreign consumption. It took us a lot of time to know what the world markets required. It makes no difference to us as to how well we know our clients. What really matters is whether they like our products or not.

"(Whatever it is), I always try to keep everything as Thai as possible. Quite a considerable amount of my time is (usually) spent at the National Museum doing research on designs."

He expounded, "I must say that silk in itself portrays a great deal of glamour. It has an aura of exotic mystery and richness about it. For centuries, it has been the fabric of kings and queens. From the way our sales are moving, I can safely say that our customers are beginning to dress like royalty."

Nobility aside, Jim also believed in man's right to work, his right to earn a profit and his right to choose the kind of work he favored. To a large extent, nearly everyone who was engaged in the industry benefited from this philosophy.

Jim's first dealing with a weaver was in 1948. Nineteen years later, that same man was still working for him. Instead of using one loom, the weaver had more than a hundred. For his contribution, the company paid him and his workers well over US$20,000 per month. But he was not an exceptional case. The seventy-one other families who had contracts with the company also earned equally good incomes. In return, they provided work for no less than three thousand other weavers.

Chapter Four

Jim was unlike any other figure in Southeast Asia. He was an American, an ex-architect, a retired army officer, a one-time spy, a silk merchant, a millionaire and a renowned collector of antiques. Most of his treasures, if not all, were amassed since the day he first came to Thailand. As time slipped by, his assortment outgrew its surroundings and this left him with not much of a choice but to find a suitable place to house them. For quite some time he toyed with the idea of constructing a dwelling which was quite unlike any other in the region. Apart from serving as his place of residence, it also had to double up as a repository for his artifacts. It was a tall order, no doubt, but he managed to achieve it nevertheless. Using parts of old up-country houses – some as old as a hundred and twenty years – he succeeded in completing his 'House on the Klong' in 1959. It was basically a colony of six traditional houses which were reassembled into his much larger place of abode. The units were dismantled and brought over via river from the ancient Thai capital of Ayutthaya. On arrival, they were carefully offloaded and pieced together. Of the six, three were left untouched.

In his quest for authenticity, he saw to it that the imposing structures were elevated a full floor above the ground. During the construction stage, he added his own touches to the buildings by positioning, for instance, a central staircase indoors rather than having it outside. Along the way, he also reversed the wall panels in his home so that it now faced inside instead of it having an external orientation.

While the final outcome of his domicile may not have been as what one would expect traditionally, it could be taken that Jim had a certain fondness for it. After he was through with its creation, he went ahead and filled his home with the items which he had collected over the

Solved!

years. Scattered about his rooms were scores of Chinese blue-and-white Ming pieces, Belgian glass, Cambodian stone figures, Victorian chandeliers, five-colored Bencharong, Thai stone images, Burmese statues and a dining table which was once used by King Rama V of Thailand.

In all, his mammoth 'House on the Klong' took up close to a hectare in area. The garden around the habitation was nothing short of a lush, well-kept mini-jungle. On it stood a typical Thai spirit house.

It took Jim almost a year to put his house in order. On completion, it turned out to be an architectural masterpiece. The press were quick to describe it as "one of the wonders of the East". In several ways, they were right: till today, it stands out as one of Bangkok's most charming attractions. His residence, which is open to the public, is presently situated near Klong Maha Nog at the end of Soi Kasemsong II, which is, incidentally, just across from the Thai National Stadium on Rama I Road.

Practically every night there was a dinner guest at his home. Hollywood stars, entrepreneurs, novelists and politicians – they all came visiting at his museum-like home. Some of the many who came by to see him included personalities such as Henry Ford II, William Fulbright, Cecil Beaton, Truman Capote, Lyndon Johnson, Ethel Merman, Adlai Stevenson, Tennessee Williams, Katherine Hepburn, Barbara Hutton, Robert Kennedy, Ann Baxter and even Prince Michael of Greece. Somerset Maugham once wrote to him after having dinner at his place: "Jim, you not only have beautiful things but what is more rare, you have displayed them beautifully."

Contrary to popular belief, Jim's circle of friends did not center merely on the rich and famous. It included, among others, those who had no particular social standing or tourists who used to stop at his shop. Whoever or whatever they were, he was always on hand to see to it that they were merrily entertained. Outwardly, many a guest found him to be a warm and compassionate person. Inwardly, very few were well aware of his deep loneliness and his desire to be loved. On the whole, he was an approachable person. It was not only a joy conversing with him; equally interesting, he was also a good listener. However, he did have a weakness, a weakness which no one dared to talk about, namely, his fuming temper. If he felt that he was being belittled, he would respond by telling off the offender. If he felt he was being made out to be someone who was not at all trustworthy, he would retaliate in extreme terms by not talking to the person.

Edward Roy De Souza

In spite of his wealth, Jim was, in very many ways, a simple man. His dressing was in no way outlandish. As for food, he was no gourmet. It could be said that he was, by nature, a caring person. Many who knew him well benefited from his kind-heartedness. The local School for the Blind was one fine example. On the quiet, he saw to it that enough funds were sent its way.

While his silk business continued to grow, so too did his popularity. The press were continually at his heels. It was just that they found him hard to resist. He could have avoided them had he wanted to but he never did. Over time, his reputation grew to legendary proportions and, with this, he came to be known by many names. Of the many, two stood out among the rest: the foreign media was fond of addressing him as 'The Thai Silk King'; the Thai press, on the other hand, coined the phrase 'The Thai Silk Millionaire'. There is no doubt that he did have a million dollars but, it was not from his business; it was actually from an inheritance. Prior to his ceasing to be seen, his annual income was close to US$33,000. For quite some time, he did own a total of eighteen per cent of his company's shares. To a certain degree, the dividends derived from his shares did help to augment his income but this did not last for very long. As the years went by, his share in the company began to shrink. This had nothing to do with poor management; it had a lot to do with his exchanging them for the favors which came his way.

Solved!

Chapter Five

There is no doubt that Jim was, in very many ways, responsible for bringing the Thai silk industry to the forefront. It started off with nothing new; over time, Thai silk, which was unknown to the outside world, grew in both demand and popularity. Jim was especially proud of his contribution; it gave him a deep sense of joy and accomplishment. However, his success came with a price. To a large extent, it drained him.

His friends and business associates were well aware of the fact that his work was slowly beginning to have an effect on his health. Out of good cheer, they encouraged him to take a break. He did so.

On Friday, March 24, 1967, he and Mrs. Constance Mangskau, 59, took the occasion to holiday at Malaysia's Cameron Highlands. Located on the northwestern tip of Pahang, the outpost is one of Malaysia's most extensive hill stations. It is about fifty kilometers off the main Kuala Lumpur-Ipoh-Butterworth road at Tapah, Perak. It may sound strange but it is true: the sanctuary is not at all easy to pinpoint on any map. This is due to the fact that the neighborhood's dwellings tend to occupy whatever land area that is readily available along the main road.

The Highlands has long been a favorite stopover for the many who want to escape from the heat of the lowlands. It got its name from William Cameron, a British surveyor who was commissioned by the then colonial government to map out the area in 1885. In a statement concerning his mapping expedition, William mentioned that he saw "a vortex in the mountains, while for a (reasonably) wide area we have gentle slopes and plateau land".

When approached, the late Sir Hugh Low, the Resident of Perak, expressed the wish of developing the flat terrain as a "sanatorium,

Solved!

health resort and open farmland". But it was not until twenty years later that the first pioneers managed to find their way to the top of 'Cameron's Land'. They were soon followed by tea planters and vegetable growers who found the fertile soil, good drainage and cool climate to be especially suitable for the growing of their crops.

The resort, which is nestled at an altitude of about 1,600 to 2,000 meters, is basically made up of three distinct villages, namely, Ringlet (jungle tree), Tanah Rata (flat land) and Brinchang (open farmland). All three are separated from one another by quite a considerable distance.

Ringlet, which is about fifty kilometers from the turn-off at Tapah, is the first stop of the district. It does boast of a number of fine places to stay in but most fun-seekers prefer to move north where there is more to see. But the journey to the top is not as easy as one would make it out to be. The road is not only narrow; it is also just as winding as well. Negotiating its endless array of hairpin bends is indeed a skill in itself.

About fourteen kilometers away is the other Highland town of Tanah Rata. It has a population of no more than 7,000, most of whom are engaged in the hospitality business. Apart from sweet-smelling dahlias, roses, tulips and chrysanthemums, the hamlet is also noted for being the prime center for a wide range of social and recreational activities.

Further up is the province of Brinchang where rows of vegetable farms form part of the picturesque landscape. It is approximately five kilometers from Tanah Rata and is one of the highest points in Malaysia which is accessible by car. Like Tanah Rata, Brinchang has an extensive assortment of hotels and eating outlets to pick and choose from. Quite close to the top of its highest peak is a radio and television station. During fair weather, one can easily get a good glimpse of the Straits of Malacca which is located to the west of the retreat.

On the whole, the Highlands can be considered as a world in miniature. It occupies the smallest constituency in Pahang, taking up an area of around 448 square kilometers. To the north, its boundary touches that of Kelantan; to the west, it shares part of its border with Perak. During the day, the temperature seldom soars above 25°C. At night, it is quite the opposite: the temperature can sometimes drop to as low as 3°C. The cool climate makes it an ideal place for tea to be grown. The growing of tea had its beginnings in 1926 when the British started the first plantations with saplings brought over from India. Today, there are no less than five established tea estates at the haven.

Apart from tea, the moorland is also noted for its insect life, jungle tracks, waterfalls, soaring peaks, scenic spots and last but not least, its awe-inspiring natives. The natives or aborigines are basically jungle dwellers. Approximately 100,000 people in peninsula Malaysia come under the general classification of 'Orang Asli'. It is actually an all-encompassing term which is used to describe the different ethnic groups such as the Batek, Chewong, Jah Hut, Jakun, Jehai, Jengjeng, Kensiu, Kentaq Bong, Lanoh, Mabetisek, Medrique, Mintil, Mos, Orang Kanaq, Orang Selitar, Sabum, Semaq Beri, Semnam, Semai, Semelai, Temiar, Temoq, Temuan and Tonga. The social structure of these groups is unique in the sense that it hinges on the concept of avoiding conflict as far as possible. Decisions within the tribe are usually made during collective discussions and the role of the chief is strictly that of a mediator.

The traditional weapon which an aborigine is allowed to own is that of a blowpipe. It is actually a tube-like structure which is made from bamboo. The length of the pipe varies according to one's taste or fancy. By force of the breath, poison darts are discharged from it.

The aborigines of the region are believed to have migrated into the area long before the arrival of the Malays. On the surface, their lifestyle has always been made out to be both primitive and backward. But this has gradually changed over the years. While many have left to take up employment and residence in the nearby towns, there are still some who prefer to treat the jungle as their home. The woodlands that they live in can be considered as thick and dense but the challenges that it has to offer are indeed varied. Many who have been to the terminal have acknowledged this to be so. Jim was no exception. He found the appeal of the forest to be both irresistible and infinite. So too did his friend, Dr Tien Gi Ling, a Singaporean-Chinese chemist and Helen, his white American-born wife.

Solved!

Chapter Six

The Lings were the owners of Moonlight bungalow, a Tudor-style dwelling which is located at No. A47, Jalan Kamunting, 39000, Tanah Rata. Situated about two kilometers from Jalan Besar, the villa is actually somewhere between the townships of Tanah Rata and Brinchang.

As far as Jim and Constance were concerned, this was their third invitation to the Ling's estate. It could be said that the foursome not only got along well; by the same token, all four shared the same love and fondness for the jungle.

When they met up on Friday, their get-together did not take up very much of their time. This was due to the fact that they reached the bungalow at different times: the first to do so was Dr Ling; Jim and Constance were next; Helen, who was tied up with a business deal, arrived at eight. The trip up was no joke – they all found it to be long and taxing. After a short dinner, they agreed to call it a day.

The next morning, while the two ladies were engrossed with their conversation, Jim and Dr Ling took the occasion to explore the tropical rainforest for themselves. They were just as anxious to try out a new trail which Dr Ling had previously discovered. After the hike, they were supposed to meet up with the two ladies at a nearby club. But their afternoon plan almost turned out to be a nightmare: along the way, it became evident to the two of them that they were lost. When they failed to show up, the women became upset. For a moment, Helen did entertain the thought of wanting to contact the police. It was only after eleven that Jim managed to spot a narrow stream. He carefully traced it and in a matter of an hour or so, they were back to familiar surroundings. Both of them were just as worn out when they strolled into the club. During the hike, Dr Ling had pulled a ligament and it was obvi-

Solved!

ous that he was a bit shaken by his morning adventure. But not so for Jim. He was especially elated that the two of them got lost along the way. While he was at the clubhouse, he gave Constance, Helen and a few of his other friends a rough run down of what transpired while he and Dr Ling were in thick jungle.

When his narration came to an end, the party left the premises and made their way for Moonlight. After lunch, they agreed to have an afternoon siesta. The Lings shared a large bedroom at the very front of the building. As for Constance, she occupied a much smaller room which was quite close to theirs. In the case of Jim, he delightfully took up residence at the remaining room which was at the rear of the house.

At about 4.30pm they got up for some tea and gave the garden a brief inspection. After a short dinner, they retired to their respective rooms for a deserving rest.

The following Sunday morning, they got up early to attend a religious service at a nearby Protestant chapel. Their program for the day was to spend some time in church following which they were to adjourn for a picnic at Gunong (Mount) Brinchang. While the rest were getting themselves ready, Jim informed them that he would be taking a slow walk to the foot of the hill. He later met up with them at the Jalan Kamunting/Jalan Besar road junction and they all drove on to Tanah Rata to attend the Easter service at All Souls' Church.

When the services came to an end, they returned to their living quarters to collect a hamper which they had earlier put aside for their planned picnic. While they were at the lodge, Jim gave them a surprise by suggesting that the picnic be held in the garden instead. For a moment, the others were taken aback by his sudden change of mind. After some persuasion, they managed to win him over to their original plan.

The drive to their selected site did not take up more than thirty minutes of their time. At the picnic, it became obvious that Jim was not his usual self; he seemed to be troubled by something that had either been said or done. For a short interval, none of them was able to make out what was actually on his mind. Sensing a funny change in his character, the Lings suggested that he take a rest in the open. He declined their offer and preferred instead that their gathering be called off. Not wanting to be a further source of disappointment to him, the trio complied with his request.

They supposedly left the site at around two and got back to their provisional home at about 2.30pm. Since they had no other plans for the afternoon, it was reported that Jim chose to sit in the hall while the rest opted for their respective rooms.

A short while later, he got up and left the house. After he had gone, it later became evident that he had left his suit jacket over the back of a chair. Apart from this, he also left behind his pill box, a box of cigarettes and a lighter.

Dr Ling remembered hearing the sound of footsteps "pass by my bedroom door (at) about 3.30pm". He presumed it was Jim going out for a stroll. As such, he did not take the trouble to look out of his window to see if this was really the case.

When Jim left the house, it was alleged that no one in particular was kept informed. During his last visit to the base, which was about five years ago, it was made known that he was stung by hornets about a kilometer from Moonlight. He did then inform Constance and his other friends that he would like visit this same spot on his next trip. Whether he did so or not, no one really knows. But one thing is for sure: he did leave the chalet for a pre-dinner stroll; he failed to return by 6pm.

The Lings and Constance did not have very much to say with regards to his short absence. After six, Dr Ling got into his car and took a slow drive to the club. He had high hopes of meeting Jim along the way. He never did. On his return, he was puzzled as to where Jim could have possibly gone to; he was not seen at the clubhouse neither was he spotted by anyone that afternoon. After a short pause, Constance gave a call to Dr Einar Ammundsen, Jim's physician, to find out if Jim was with him at the Smokehouse Inn. Dr Ammundsen, who was at the tourist haunt by coincidence, told her that Jim did not come by to see him.

By now the Lings and Constance began to sense that something was obviously not right. Out of concern for his friend, Dr Ling gave a call to his rental agents and informed them of Jim's failure to return. He felt that since they knew the area rather well, word of Jim's disappearance would soon be forthcoming. This, however, did not in any way come to pass. With not much of a choice now opened to him, Dr Ling went ahead and lodged a police report.

The police were surprised that the man they had to deal with was no stranger. After filing his report, Dr Ling was assured that word of his missing friend would be filtered down to the settlements in the area. He was also informed that if Jim failed to return, the police would conduct a search for him the following morning.

On his return from the station, two visitors called at his residence: one was his rental agent, a Dutchman; the other was a British army

Solved!

major. After a short discussion, the visitors left the cottage and headed for a nearby hill. The area was briefly inspected but they drew a blank. Undaunted, the two returned to the bungalow to see if they could gather more clues about Jim's likely whereabouts. A few minutes later, they left the place and made another attempt to find for Jim at an entirely different location. But their second endeavor, like the first, proved to be fruitless.

At daybreak, about five policemen showed up at the country home. After studying Jim's passport details, they left the scene. Just after they had gone, Constance phoned Barry Cross, her son-in-law, and informed him of Jim's failure to return. When the call ended, Barry immediately notified general Black and gave him the news.

Later that morning, the police, with the help of thirty Orang Asli (aborigines), combed the area. The search was reasonably intensive but there was just no trace of Jim. Before noon, news of his disappearance began to spread. By then, more than a hundred people were on the lookout for him, to no avail.

The following day (March 28), the biggest hunt in Malaysian history was staged. The police came well-prepared to handle the task on hand. Most of the teams came complete with walkie-talkies, loud hailers and field telephones. A select group was armed with pistols and submachine guns. In the late afternoon, two British Royal Army Air Corps helicopters en route for Seremban made a stop at the depot. They were asked to assist with the hunt. After getting the necessary clearance from their immediate superiors, they did so.

The sweep of the jungle was fairly thorough. It went on without a break for most of the day. Till late in the evening, no one was able to find Jim. The police concluded that Jim could either be trapped or accidentally injured. However, they were convinced that he would somehow or other be able to find his way back. His previous jungle-survival training, they reasoned, would be sufficient to see him through whatever difficulties he was in.

Chapter Seven

On Wednesday, March 29, the police were provided with a few pointers which they found to be especially helpful in their quest to locate Jim.

Che Fatimah binte Mohamed Yeh, 24, a cook at the Lutheran Mission bungalow, told superintendent A.S. Nathan that she saw Jim on Sunday at about 4pm.

"I was in the kitchen," she said, "when I saw him come up the road. He had on a white shirt and a pair of gray slacks. He stopped for a while to take a look at the garden. While looking at the plants, he did not speak to anyone. A short while later, he left the premises and headed the same way from where he came."

In a separate report, a servant employed at the Overseas Mission Fellowship bungalow informed the police that she saw a man who looked like Jim. She said she saw him standing on a plateau which happens to be opposite the mansion. According to her, he was seen standing there at around 4pm. After thirty minutes or so, he was not to be seen.

The last person who saw him was an employee of the former Eastern Hotel (which is now known as the New Garden Inn). He was quite sure he saw someone who resembled Jim heading in the direction of the track which led to the golf course.

The police considered all three clues to be particularly useful. But the sighting of the second witness gave them the impression that Jim could have wandered over a nearby ridge. Beyond it is a forked track: one led to the dense, triple-canopy jungle; the other circled back. The police party, which was divided into several groups, did not cover this particular sector. At the start of the operation, they were of the opinion

Solved!

that it was highly unlikely of Jim to have gone in that direction. To begin with, the area is vastly impenetrable. To explore it would not only mean a waste of their time; it would also mean their having to deploy more men than necessary to look for him. But the testimony of the second witness made them think otherwise. After some deliberation, a fresh set of orders was issued for the area to be combed.

Later that afternoon, the members of the press who had gathered at Tanah Rata, were informed that plans were underway for a change in the search's leadership command. They were told that Assistant Commissioner of Police (ACP) Yusoff Khan, who was put in charge of the operation, would be recalled to Ipoh to attend to "urgent matters". Just before his departure ACP Khan took the opportunity to notify the press that the police were of the impression that "if Jim had wandered beyond the ridge, it would take several more days before he would be found".

This estimation on his part left many a resident worried of the outcome of the search. The hamlet, they reasoned, could be freezing cold at night. By virtue of the fact that he was not properly attired, most locals were of the impression that his chances of surviving were indeed slim.

Regardless of the situation that he was in, the casting about for him went on without very much of a break. At sunset, the police were told of a piece of news which they found to be rather disturbing. It was brought to their attention that a tiger was spotted a few days earlier in the vicinity of Brinchang. They were informed that two residents saw the carnivorous mammal while it was in the process of dragging away their dog. On receiving this piece of information, a portion of the three hundred strong police party was ordered to back track. Arrangements were later made for them to be re-deployed to the county's northwestern sector.

On the whole, the police found the disappearance of Jim to be somewhat puzzling. After the dinner interval, they had a hard time trying to figure out what could have possibly happened to him. It was this uncertainty that left them in a situation where they had no choice but to hold on to several unconfirmed views. Of the many, they did not rule out the possibility that he could have been kidnapped. Jim, they noted, had been to the Camerons on two or more occasions. While on vacation, he was in the habit of moving around alone. He was usually seen at the upland's lake and jungle-fringed areas. The police were suspicious that an organized gang could have kept an eye on him and taken the opportunity to kidnap him while he was all by himself. But there was a strange twist to his vanishing which left them in want of an answer. From their experience, ransoms are usually demanded within a span of forty-eight hours. Since the start of the search operation, there had been no demand for any ransom.

Ransom or no ransom, the police went on with their investigations without any sign of a let-up. By then, they had spent more than seventy-two hours looking for Jim. The hunt, which was conducted in shifts, went on round-the-clock. With the exit of ACP Khan, superintendent A.S. Nathan was put in charge of the search operation. The handing over of duties was quite smooth, there being no reported change in the mission's overall strategy.

Solved!

Chapter Eight

The sudden eclipse of Jim certainly came as a shock to many; this was especially so for those who knew him reasonably well. But they were not put off by the news that came their way. Put simply, they were quite confident that Jim would somehow surface again. One such person was Constance. According to her, they had known each other for more than twenty-two years. When queried about his character, she remembered a trip which they made to the Himalayas a few years back.

"During the trip," she said, "Jim went missing... for almost four weeks. We spent a lot of our time looking for him in the mountains. The other members of our team and I were surprised when he showed up at the end of our heartbreaking search. He was certainly weak and exhausted on his return."

"Jim," she noted, "was in the habit of losing himself. He would turn up when least expected. I have a funny feeling he was in one of his unpredictable moods when he ventured on his latest jaunt into the jungle."

Dr Ammundsen, Jim's close friend and physician, took a similarly optimistic view. He believed that there was "still hope that he might be wading downstream or down-trail. For all you know, he could eventually show up at a settlement... a few kilometers to the east or elsewhere."

In Thailand, the news of his vanishing was somewhat different: in brief, it was nothing but a mixed bag of guesses and hope. Some were resigned to conclude that he was as good as gone; others, however, were quite sure that he would ultimately return on his own. Astrologers and fortune-tellers who were consulted were of the impression that he was "still alive and that it was only a matter of time before he would be found."

Solved!

In Malaysia, the outlook amongst some of his close friends was a lot dimmer. As the days passed, they began to doubt as to whether he was still alive. "One can go on walking," they noted, "without meeting another human being in the thick of the jungle." Based on this reasoning, they were resigned to the fact that his chances of being alive were indeed slim.

In Bangkok, the Thai Silk Company took the news of his disappearance more seriously. The officials of the company were positive that something amiss could have happened to him while he was on leave at the hideaway. Charles U. Sheffield, 40, who was appointed acting manager, announced that "a generous reward (of US$10,000) will be paid by the Thai Silk Company to any person or persons" who succeeded in finding Jim. The offer was made on Wednesday, March 29, that is, three days after he was declared as lost. This incentive was a close follow-up to the strong rumors in the Thai capital that he could have been kidnapped and taken to another country.

Apart from this, two other enticements were also declared. On her part, Constance affirmed that she was more than willing to hand out a gift to anyone who knew where her friend could be found. She left the details of her "handsome reward" with the police at Tanah Rata. The Malaysian police, in line with tradition, also came up with a remuneration amounting to RM10,000 (about US$3,000). The payment, which was approved by the inspector general of police, was valid for a period of three months.

The day after the Thai Silk Company announced their reward, a young lady showed up at the company's premises and informed the staff that she knew something about Jim's predicament. Determined to give anything a try, they ushered her into a dimly lit room. A collection of candles and joss sticks were lit and placed under a white piece of cloth. While she was concentrating on her prayers, the anxious employees kept their focus on the fabric which was hung on the wall. They were confident that the 'screen' would somehow show them something about the situation that Jim was in. To their great disappointment, they saw nothing. But their guest swore she saw something. When asked what it was, she said she saw Jim being held captive by two gunmen. All three were in the jungle.

Over at Tanah Rata, a *ton-kee* (medium) who was consulted for his assistance came up with a vastly different interpretation. Thong Weng, 29, a part-time house painter from Brinchang, proclaimed to two of his followers that Jim was "alive but possessed by evil spirits". Prior to his declaring this to Shee Voon Chin, a sundry-shop proprietor and Raymond Chan, a food contractor, he reportedly went into a number of trances. His first was on Wednesday, March 29. After coming out of his trance, he predicted that Jim would return to the chateau "on his own". He also mentioned that this would take place "at about 9am the next day". But nothing of that sort came to pass. Not to be outdone, he spent the later part of the morning working himself into a double trance. He pleaded with the spirit world for a positive hint as to where Jim could be traced. In all, it took him more than an hour to come out of his spell.

After regaining his normal senses, he confidently declared to Voon Chin and Raymond that "Jim is still being possessed by evil spirits". He went on to say that Jim could be found "in a hole under a large tree which is not far from the bungalow." He said, "During their search, a few police parties did pass by this spot without noticing him. He tried to call out to them but, being weak, his calls went unheard."

On hearing this, Voon Chin and Raymond got together some of their employees to conduct a survey of their own. Armed with gongs and cymbals, they took the route which Thong Weng had instructed them to do. Their scanning of the woods was quite thorough. They took a vigilant note of the large trees along the way. Their bases were carefully checked for holes. Depressions that were covered in thick ground cover were not only checked but also double-checked. Overall, the group spent about two hours looking for him. By noon they gave up and returned to the temple. They approached Thong Weng and asked him why they were unable to spot Jim while strictly adhering to whatever he had earlier told them to do. When pressed for an answer, Thong Weng was quick to point out that they all went in the wrong direction. To satisfy their needs, he went into another trance. He later led the group for a brief inspection of the jungle. The result of their exploration was nothing but a heartbreaking blank. He later told a police source that he would be heading for Ipoh to consult a "higher medium". He did promise to return with a firm answer. He never did.

Whatever the mystic predicted, the police generally took no notice of it. Their attention was more focused on empirical evidence of the likely areas where Jim could be found. During their air and ground mission on March 29, the pilot of an RMAF helicopter enquired of the aboriginal settlers as to whether they had come into contact with the missing man. They informed him that they did not. Before leaving, the pilot left

Solved!

word with them to keep the police informed if they encountered Jim. He also reminded them not to harm him.

While the pilot hop scotched from one settlement to another, on the ground were no less than a hundred and sixty officers and men who went about scouring the rainforest. Their senses were alert for any sign that may give them a clue to Jim's whereabouts. Led by Assistant Superintendent of Police (ASP) Sarain Singh, they returned in the afternoon without any success.

When interviewed by the press, ASP Singh had this to say: "There is no new development today. But we're still hopeful."

The police were hopeful, no doubt, but two groups lost hope along the way. The first were the volunteers from the British army; the other were the students from the Dalat American School. Both parties called off their hunt after the lunch break.

Later in the afternoon there was a slight change in events: Dr Ling left the district for Singapore; at Moonlight, Helen and Constance continued to wait for Jim's return. They wanted to take care of him in the event that he showed up. Helen informed the media that she took the view that, "despite the dim prospects, everything must be all right with him. We will remain here to see the end of this search. We will be here for as long as we know and believe he will come through safe."

Constance was just as confident in her outlook. But she was upset when told that a number of soothsayers were consulted to help trace her long-time friend.

"My Catholic faith," she said, "does not allow for belief in human beings having supernatural powers."

"It's utter rubbish, poppy-cock!" she exploded, when told that a medium had predicted that Jim was "safe but weak".

"My faith is in God," she reasoned, "and it is this faith in God that will see Jim through as well."

Chapter Nine

Dr Ling got back to Singapore the following day. Just after he arrived at his home, he received a call from a man who identified himself as Michael Ian Vermont. He told Dr Ling he had some information with regards to Jim's whereabouts. He asked if he could meet up with Dr Ling to see if they could discuss the subject a little further. Without any hesitation, Dr Ling agreed.

When he arrived at Dr Ling's residence, the visitor seemed a bit nervous. After gaining his composure, he informed Dr Ling that Jim was being kept at a house in Tapah. He added that if Dr Ling was prepared to accompany him to the municipality, the two of them could look into Jim's possible release.

Dr Ling was very much for the idea but because of his work commitments, he was unable to go up to Tapah with Michael. He suggested instead that Michael meet up with two of his other friends. Michael agreed. But the mistake which Michael made was to ask Dr Ling for some money. He stated that he needed the money so that he could travel up to Tapah. Out of goodwill, Dr Ling gave him the equivalent of US$15.

Immediately after Michael had left, Dr Ling gave a call to Helen and informed her of his recent meeting. Following this, brigadier general Edwin Black and Dean Frasche, two close friends of the Lings, were also kept informed. Both the general and Dean were for the idea of meeting up with Michael. But when they were at Tapah, Michael failed to show up. The next day, he gave a call to Helen and apologized to her for not being able to keep his appointment. While conversing with her, he suggested that another date be fixed. From the tone of his voice, Helen could sense that "he was up to something which was no good".

Solved!

To satisfy her curiosity, she asked him for his full name and Singaporean identification card number. He willingly gave them to her but a check with the relevant authorities revealed that his name and number were not in their register.

After this incident, "Michael" was neither heard of nor seen by the Lings. But it was only for "a very short while". Some time later he surfaced again. This time around, he took on a more aggressive stance. He occasionally gave them a call and reminded them to "get out of the country".

Initially, the Lings were troubled by his frequent threats. But as time went by, they learnt to take no notice of it.

Chapter Ten

Over at Tanah Rata, there was a noticeable change in mood as far as the scouting for Jim was concerned. The operation, which was now in its seventh day, began to gain momentum when it became obvious that brigadier general Edwin Black, the chief of the American support forces in Thailand, would be joining in the hunt.

Before coming over to the resort, the military leader kept in touch with a religious figure to ascertain if he could provide useful insights as to where Jim could be found. The soothsayer, a reasonably popular figure in Bangkok, did specify in one of his free-circulating pamphlets that:

"Wishful thinking is the dowser's greatest enemy. If he is bent on finding water at a certain spot the pendulum will turn, the stick will pull down on that spot, and most probably he will be wrong in the prognostications.

"Suppose a plane crashes between Rangoon and Bangkok, in the Tenasserim range – and that is a very bad place to crash – a good dowser will point out on the map the exact place where the plane is, and how many people still survive, and how many are wounded. It goes without saying that those indications may occasionally prove highly useful..."

Useful or not, the general complied with whatever the clairvoyant had advised. To make it a lot easier for him, the army officer handed him a detailed map of the region. After taking a good look at it, the mystic pointed to a particular spot and encouraged the commander to concentrate his probe on the area which he had highlighted. Equipped with this information, general Black came to the territory with his aide, lieutenant Dennis Horgan and his long-time friend, Dean Frasche. The first thing they did was to visit the address where Jim had stayed. While they were at the double-storied house, Helen and Constance were repeated-

Solved!

ly asked about the developments which unfolded prior to the unexplained absence of their friend. Of the two, Constance certainly had a lot more to say.

The threesome were told that just before their coming over to stay with the Lings, Jim and Constance had spent a day in Penang. Since Jim was especially tied up with a lot of last-minute details, it was Constance who took the trouble to finalize their travel arrangements.

When they met up at the airport on Thursday, it became evident to the two of them that Jim was not in line with two statutory requirements. In the first instance, he had failed to get his compulsory cholera inoculation. Apart from this, he had also forgotten to obtain his clearance certificate to show he had no outstanding tax payments with the country's Inland Revenue department. By right, he was not at all supposed to leave the country. Fortunately, Constance knew some of the officials rather well and this helped to smoothen out the irregularities.

The couple left Bangkok as planned and got in to Penang in the afternoon. She recollected that "neither of us had been there before and we were anxious to see the island (for ourselves)." She added: "We hired a car and (while we) were driving around the island... Jim became anxious to return to Georgetown to get a haircut." Constance admitted that she was put off with Jim's unexpected request. She later dropped him off at a barbershop while they were on their way to the Ambassador Hotel where they had earlier booked two rooms for their short outing.

When Jim returned, Constance remembered him commenting that he would have rather that they had stayed at the Eastern & Oriental hotel instead of the Ambassador because it was an old colonial establishment which had much the same feel as The Oriental in Bangkok. Constance was unable to make out why this was brought up in the very first place. She never did venture to ask him and it was left as that.

Later that day, the two of them had a quiet dinner at an Indian restaurant, after which they went for an evening stroll. The following morning they got up early, booked a taxi and made their way to the province. While they were on their way to the mainland, the driver of the taxi suddenly stopped his vehicle and left them for about five minutes. He later returned with a relief driver who took over the driving from him.

Apart from this development, they also encountered another change just before they got over to the prefecture. This happened at Tapah where they not only had to deal with a change of drivers but a change of vehicles as well. The next taxi which they were told to board had two

Chinese passengers waiting in it. Jim and Constance were totally against the idea of sharing the ride with the other two commuters. After some deliberation, the other two travelers were asked to get off and the driver saw to it that they were driven on their own to the outpost.

Satisfied with whatever that was brought up, general Black and his team later got together to work out the details of their plan.

The subsequent morning, the threesome got up early and made the necessary arrangements for an aerial tower to be positioned on a water tank near the country house. The device was designed to throw a radar communication 'net' which covered a radius of approximately sixteen kilometers. Lieutenant Horgan was put in charge of the tower and his role was to ensure that a minute-by-minute radio contact was established with his superior's exploration team.

General Black, who was equipped with a portable wireless set, went into the woods to conduct a survey of his own. He was in constant contact with his aide while being accompanied by Dean and two aborigines. Apart from being able to keep in touch with his assistant, general Black was also able to establish radio contact with the other parties who were on the lookout for Jim.

The search conducted on Saturday, April 1, was indeed extensive. Joining in the exploration were two hundred more officers and men from Perak's police field force. They were earlier engaged in a training operation at Tambun near Ipoh. They came to Tanah Rata from Tanjung Rambutan after making their way through the jungle. They were later ordered to merge with the various police parties who were based at the administrative division.

Just before the lunch break, a twelve-year-old boy who proclaimed he knew where Jim could be found came forward to share his knowledge with the police. Mustada bin Yahaya, a *kramat hidup* (living spirit) told the police that Jim had moved from the state of Pahang to the neighboring state of Kelantan. He said through his father, Yahaya bin Ahmad Hashim, 63, that it was pointless to look for Jim at the holiday camp. His father, a farmer, informed the police that his son's services were strictly voluntary. He added that the subject of money would not be discussed unless Jim was discovered based on his son's revelation.

The police, however, did not pay much attention to the boy's observations. After the lunch break, the area around the detached home was backtracked. The sweep of the jungle was later extended to the haven's north and northeast. By late evening, most of the assigned parties were

Solved!

back at their command post. Throughout their mission, they came across no sign or trace of the absent man.

The following day, there was no let up in their pursuit of Jim: the police carried on with their winnowing from where they had earlier left off; general Black and his crew went about with a separate probe of their own. The Sunday exploration, though intensive, proved to be no more of a success than before.

The morning after, general Black and his team informed the police that they were calling off their investigations. They left the scene and got over to Kuala Lumpur on the same day. While resting at the Malaysian capital, the general told a group of reporters that "there has been absolutely no trace of Jim's whereabouts." "Jim," he said, "has a knowledge of jungle law. This would have enabled him to survive for a few days. On realizing that he was lost, he would have been on the lookout for a stream. He would have subsequently followed it expecting to come to a village.

"I find his disappearance rather strange. There has not been a single clue, not a bit of torn clothing or even a shoe. According to the police here, a ransom is usually demanded within a time frame of forty-eight hours. Nothing of that sort has surfaced since the day he went missing."

Having said that, general Black and Dean returned to Bangkok. As for lieutenant Horgan, it is assumed he stayed on in Kuala Lumpur for a short while before making his way for the United States.

Meanwhile, at Moonlight, Helen and Constance, who had extended their stay at the habitation, left the area for Singapore on April 5. Helen was especially thankful to the authorities for assigning inspector Tan Ai Bee to look after her and Constance. She was also grateful to the police for trying their best to locate her missing friend.

The morning after their departure, there was no slow down in the search for Jim: the police went on with their hunt. A party comprising fifty men left Tanah Rata and headed more than eight kilometers into the jungle. Two RMAF helicopters were also on hand to assist them in their pursuit but no signs of Jim were found.

In the afternoon, a nine-man team led by businessman Yip Wah Swee entered the jungle near Moonlight to conduct an investigation of their own. They were determined to look for Jim at a particular hill. Before heading for the vicinity, Wah Swee told a few reporters that he had met a 'higher medium' from Bidor, Perak. The soothsayer informed him that Jim was still alive and that he could be found on a knoll which is not far from the lodge. According to Wah Swee, the seer notified him that, "Jim is on top of a hill from which all the search parties had turned their backs after checking its foot." He was told that all he had to do was to go up to the summit and bring him down. But before doing so, it was required of him to fire two packets of firecrackers. The purpose was to scare away the evil spirits who were residing in and around the area.

Wah Swee had tremendous faith in whatever the mystic had instructed him to do. On reaching the site, he and the members of his group fired two packets of firecrackers. After the smoke had cleared, they eagerly made their way to the top. When they reached the peak, their excitement turned into disappointment: Jim was not at all to be found. Crestfallen, all nine got off from the mount.

Solved!

Chapter Eleven

The hunt for Jim went on uninterruptedly for eleven days. On their part, the police did put in a concerted effort to track him down. On the twelfth day, there was a noticeable downsizing in their operation: more than two hundred officers and men were ordered to leave the neighborhood and head back for their home base in Perak. Only a skeleton force numbering less than a hundred were instructed to stay behind.

Over in Thailand, the situation was a lot different. The Thai Silk Company, which was monitoring developments closely, announced that the US$10,000 reward for the finder of Jim would be raised by another US$2,500. George Barrie, Jim's close acquaintance and business associate, was the one who came up with the additional offer.

Jim or no Jim, the Thai Silk Company went on to function in much the same way as it previously did. In an exclusive interview with the press, Charles U. Sheffield said, "Until we hear from him, we will just continue producing and selling silk the way we've always done. There is no doubt we would not be able to find someone to replace him as a designer. He has been into designing for fifteen years. Some of his designs are classics and some of these are still being sold today.

"If he does not turn up we would have no choice but to find another designer to replace him. He would have to be someone who has much the same feel as Jim. Whatever the outcome, there would not be much of a change in the overall policy of the company. For the time being, we do not want to make any quick changes in the company's general set-up. We believe there is still a good possibility that he will be found."

The clueless search continued. For days on end, the jungles were criss-crossed. Cries of "Jim! Jim!" drew no response. With the dwindling of the police field force, the casting about for him took on an

Solved!

entirely different twist – the seekers narrowed down to two categories: the first were experts who knew the jungle like the back of their hands; the second were those who delved into the supernatural. Both parties were just as confident of success. Put simply, they were more than eager to go out of their way to track Jim down.

The first to do so was Awan bin Osman. He went into the jungle on the morning of Thursday, April 20. A few hours later, he emerged from the woods with a worried look on his face. When sought for his views, the *bomoh* (witch doctor) was quick to say that Jim "did not go into the jungle at all". He later told a number of reporters that he needed more time to reflect on the kind of situation that Jim was in. A week slipped by. Then two. After that, nothing more was heard of from him.

On Sunday, April 23, Richard Noone, 49, a British planning officer with the Southeast Asia Treaty Organization (SEATO) came onto the scene. He was no stranger to the jungles of the area. At one stage, he served as head of the Malayan Department of Aborigines.

After two days of careful planning, Richard, a Cambridge-trained anthropologist, went into the woods with two assistants. Both helpers were equally at home in any tropical rainforest: one was a border scout from Sarawak; the other was an aborigine witch doctor.

For three days, the trio went to great lengths to look for Jim. While moving around in thick jungle, they came into contact with a few aborigines but they were unable to provide the threesome with leads as to where Jim could be found. Undiscouraged, the group carried on exploring in the hope of meeting up with him from where the field force had earlier left off.

While Richard and his two partners were still in the wilderness, a controversial figure showed up at Tanah Rata. He was none other than Peter Hurkos, a private investigator from the United States. He came to the area on Tuesday, April 25 with his personal secretary, Miss Stephany Farb (now Mrs. Stephany Hurkos) and lieutenant Dennis Horgan, the aide to brigadier general Edwin Black.

While the three of them were at the Cameronian town, Peter quickly took the opportunity to make his extrasensory powers known. He told some members of the police force interesting things about their lives. A young officer, for instance, was told that prior to his reporting for duty, he made love to his wife on a kitchen table. Peter's assessment turned out to be correct.

As for the circumstances that Jim was in, Peter was sure he had an appropriate answer. While he was at the chateau, the first thing he did

Edward Roy De Souza

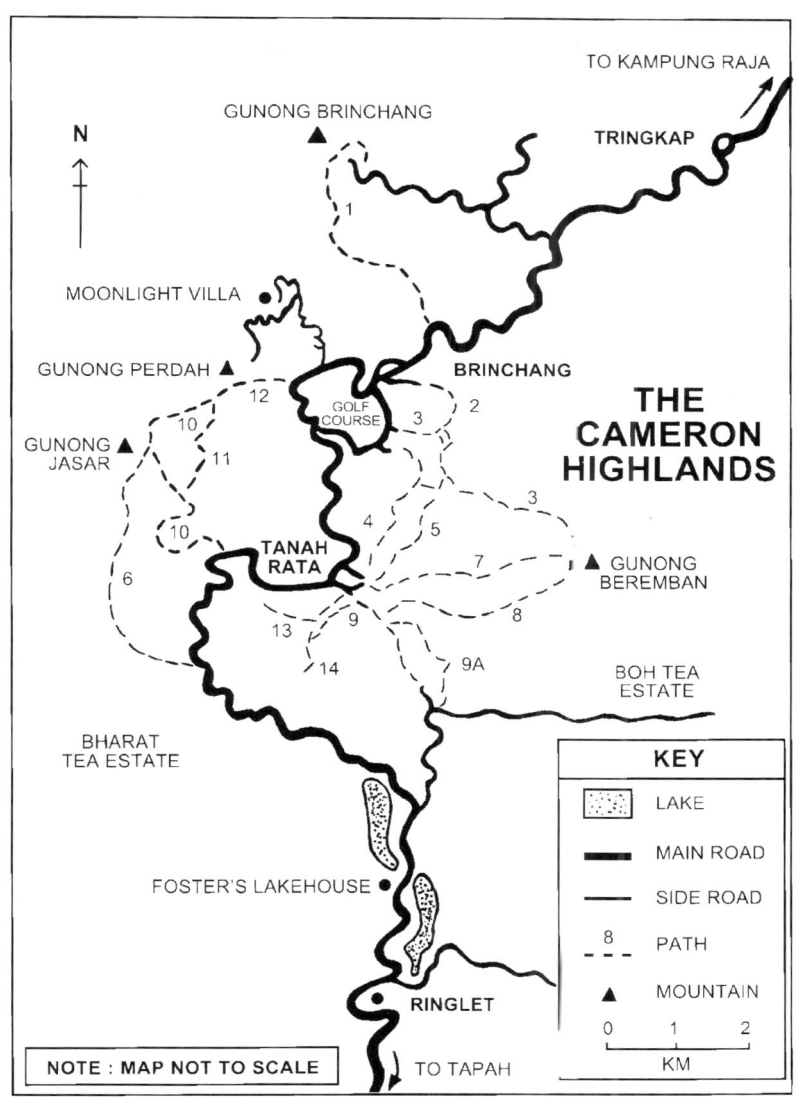

Solved!

Thong Weng... the Chinese temple medium

Mrs Mangskau... Jim's social companion

Dadi Balsara... the Indian astrologer

Jim Thompson... the legendary Thai Silk King

Lt. Horgan... the aide to Gen. Black

Che Fatimah... the Malay maid who saw Jim

Edward Roy De Souza

Mrs Ling... the owner of 'Moonlight' villa

Dr T. G. Ling... Jim's long-time friend

Gen. Black... the American commander

Peter Hurkos... the Dutch telepathy expert

Richard Noone... the British anthropologist

Pridi Panomyong... the ex-Thai prime minister

Solved!

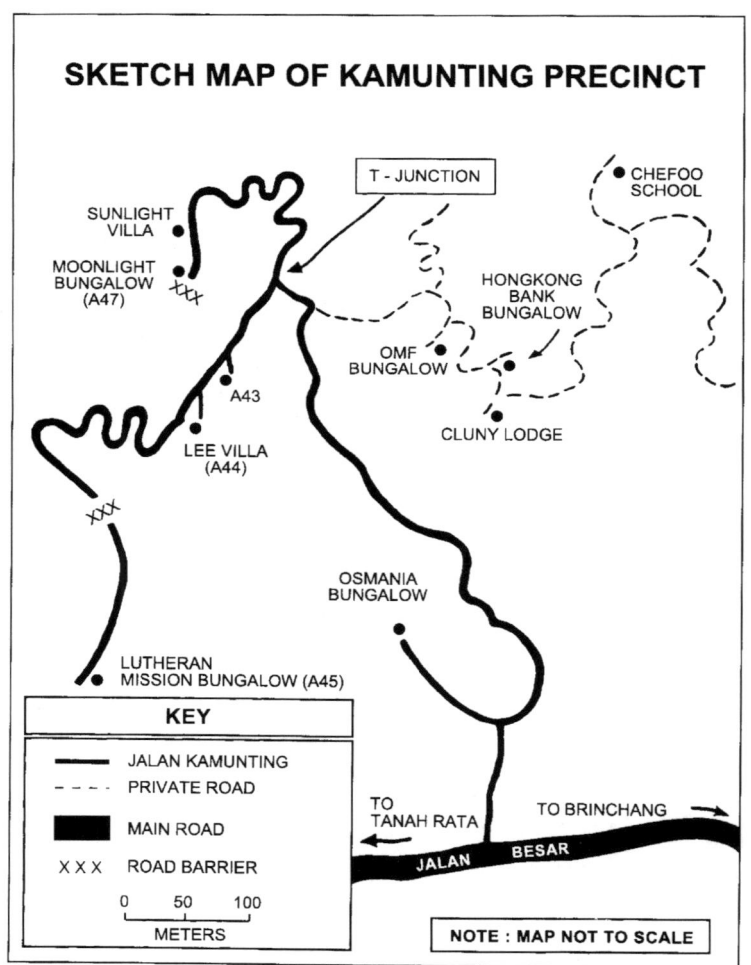

was to pace the garden in a very unusual manner. Then he stopped to feel a chair which was left at the veranda. After a short pause, he gave out a loud yell, "This is the chair! Yes, this is the chair that Jim sat on just before he disappeared!" A brief silence followed. A few minutes later, he sat down on the floor just outside the house. A photograph of Jim and two maps were laid out. The first drawing highlighted the countries which made up the continent of Asia; the second featured the details of the resort. While shifting his eyes at Jim's photograph and the two charts, his face grew tensed. Seconds later he broke out into a strange stammer. According to his secretary, he uttered the following string of words:

"He was sitting in the chair... right over there... he was not sitting in the house... the chair was on the veranda... aagh, Prebi, ooogh... Thompson... Prebi, Pridi... fourteen people... fourteen people took him... Prebe or Bebe... orah blah-lun-dah Bebe... he is not in the jungle... I want to follow the route where they picked him up... he was sitting right there... this chair... there was nobody in the room... they were upstairs... he was sitting outside in this chair... this chair... not in the jungle... car... fourteen people... one vehicle, like a military vehicle... like a truck... I see truck... ah, truck, about from here on the road... he walks down the road... somebody woke him up... he was sitting outside and somebody came in here... a friend of his... Bebe or Prebie... Pridi has own army... no bandits... nothing to do with bandits... he walks about half a mile, with Bebe or Prebie... truck on the road... fourteen people... one person here, one person picked him up... he knows him... he was sitting on the veranda and the men came in... asked for something, I don't know... he went down the road... got chloroform... chloroform... sleep in truck..."

After returning to his normal self, Peter did state, "it is ridiculous to look for Jim at the Highlands or even within a-hundred-and-sixty kilometer radius of it".

"There is no way that you'll find him there," he said. "It's just that he had been abducted to another country. You can take it from me that he is not being held for ransom. I am prepared to stake my neck on this!"

Peter was positive that fourteen members of an underground communist movement took Jim away after knocking him out with chloroform. Jim, he claimed, met a man in civilian clothes while he was sitting at the veranda. He got up to greet the man. A short while later, the two of them left the residence and took a walk down the road. After clearing a distance of about a kilometer, Jim was rendered unconscious with a dose of chloroform. Immediately after this, thirteen men dressed

Solved!

in military attire came out of their hiding places and carried him to a waiting truck. Within minutes, he was transferred to a nearby river where a waiting boat brought him to another state. Much later, his kidnappers saw to it that he was quietly smuggled into Cambodia.

After completing his assessment, Peter left the resort and made his way for Bangkok where he met up with a Buddhist monk named Keo. During their brief encounter, they were in complete agreement that Jim was being detained in Cambodia for political reasons. Just before their meeting came to an end, the Thai mystic predicted that Jim would come out in the open and have something to say about the war in Vietnam. He envisaged that this would take place on or before June 15.

After his get-together with Keo, Peter and his secretary left the country for home. Prior to their heading for Bangkok, Peter was asked by several concerned parties as to how he acquired his talent for extrasensory perception. To satisfy their curiosity he said, "I am a Christian (Roman Catholic). My work as a telepathy expert has nothing to do with showmanship. It is (actually) a gift from God."

But while he was at the refuge, he left one aspect of his stammering unanswered, that is, the similar sounding names of Prebi and Pridi. Many who were keeping close tabs on Jim's visionary recapitulation took it that he was obviously referring to Pridi Panomyong, the ex-prime minister of Thailand.

There is no question that Pridi was indeed a colorful figure in Thai politics. In 1932, during a *coup d'etat*, Pridi was appointed to serve as the People's Party's chief driving force. Around that time, the worldwide economic crisis had a considerable effect on Thailand's rice exports. To correct the unfavorable situation, the country's monarch, King Prajadhipok, was persuaded by his council of advisers to drop the gold standard which linked the Thai baht to the British pound. But, by the time he did so, the country's financial situation took a turn for the worse. The government was then left with not much of a choice but to reduce the wages of its junior staff members. This led to widespread discontentment. For the next few months, rumors were rampant that Prajadhipok would be the last regal representative of Thailand. In April 1932, he presided over the grand pageantry which featured a royal barge procession in Bangkok. Two months later, a *coup d'etat* brought his paternal but absolute rule to an end. The coup was staged by the People's Party which was made up of representatives from the military and a number of civilians.

On the military side, captain Luang Pibulsongram (Pibul) managed to garner the support of the army to form a separate political front of his own. With a few tanks, he initiated a 'revolution' which subsequently led to the 'capture' of the city. Apart from this, he also succeeded in holding several members of the royal family as hostages.

At the time of the 'uprising', King Prajadhipok was not in his homeland. When news of the coup reached him, he quickly returned to Bangkok. To avoid a scene of carnage, he accepted the provisional constitution by which he "ceased to rule but continued to reign". This marked the end of absolute monarchy in Thailand; it was now replaced by party dictatorship.

Once in power, the administration was quick to declare that the locals were not educated enough to rule themselves. As such, the incoming government's first ten years of rule was to be taken as a trial period for democracy to be properly introduced into the country. In December 1932, King Prajadhipok was made to sign a newly enacted Parliamentary Constitution which called for a general election to be held once in every four years.

A year later, the administration became divided by Pridi's style of government which advocated the nationalization of all land under cultivation. His policy was viewed by many as being typically communistic and this forced him out of office. The following year, a counter-coup took place and this brought about a reshuffling of the members in the Executive Council during which Pibul gained ascendancy. For the next twenty years, Thai politics was dominated by either Pibul or Pridi. Pibul, who became a general, had the full backing of the military; Pridi, on the other hand, had the support of the nation's intelligentsia.

While power see-sawed between Pibul and Pridi, King Prajadhipok found his new role increasingly uncomfortable. His differences with the regime resulted in his abdication of the throne in 1935. When he died in 1941, Ananda Mahidol, his ten-year-old nephew, was proclaimed king. A Regency Council was formed and Pridi was appointed to serve as regent to the young king who was at that time studying in Switzerland.

For the next three years, the country had to put up with a series of political upheavals. Pibul took advantage of the uneasy political situation to strengthen his control over the country.

A few years later, a pro-Allied underground resistance group, the *Seri Thai* or Free Thai Movement, emerged. During the Japanese

Solved!

Occupation, it received the full support of Pridi who was then regent to Ananda. The group was trained in Sri Lanka with the aim of carrying out clandestine activities against the Japanese. When the Japanese surrendered in 1945, Pibul's collaborative government came to an end. Seni Pramoj, a politician based in the United States, was appointed to serve as Prime Minister. But his premiership did not last for very long. A few months later, Pridi took over. That same year, Ananda Mahidol returned to Thailand. Just a year later, the young king was reportedly shot dead while he was in his room. Many were of the opinion that Pridi had a hand in the crime. To avoid getting himself into any trouble, he left the country.

There was one theory which immediately surfaced concerning Peter's repetitive mentioning of Pridi. Many took it that it was Pridi who met Jim while he was sitting at the veranda. After a short exchange of words, both of them left the rural home and made their way to the main road. After covering a distance of about a kilometer, Pridi knocked him out with a bout of chloroform. Following this, thirteen men came out of their hiding places and carried him to a waiting truck. Being a Sunday, Pridi instructed the driver to avoid the busier roads. The under-utilized roads to the golf course were used instead. Pridi then saw to it that Jim was put on a waiting boat and brought over to another state. He then made arrangements for Jim to be sneaked out of the country into Cambodia.

But why did Pridi have to do such a thing? The commonly held view was that Pridi was anxious to make a political comeback. He had no one else to turn to but Jim. When he brought this up to Jim, Jim was very much against the idea. Fearing that Jim would leak his plans, Pridi took no chances, knocked Jim out with chloroform, and later saw to it that Jim was got rid off.

In the Thai scheme of things, many were quite at ease in accepting this theory for what it was made out to be. But when confronted, Pridi readily denied being involved in such a development. When pressed, he even went to the extent of providing evidence to show that he was never in Malaysia at the time of Jim's announced disappearance.

With this theory demolished, another speculation took center stage. A number of pressmen were of the view that a communist agent met Jim while he was sitting all by himself at the veranda. The communist leader, who was known to him, approached him and asked him to accompany him down the road. While the two of them were taking a walk, the leader injected him with a portion of chloroform. Within minutes, Jim became unconscious. He was then put into a military truck and brought to a riverbank where a standby vessel was used to transfer him to another state. It was here that Chin Peng, the former head of the outlawed Communist Party of Malaya, took custody of him. When the time was right, he saw to it that Jim was flown in to Cambodia. While in Cambodia, the plan was for Jim to be brainwashed and used by the communists to exert pressure on the Americans. In the late 1960s, the war in Vietnam was reaching its climax. The Americans used Thailand as a springboard to launch their air attacks on Hanoi. To put a check on this advantage, the communists had to think of a way of outsmarting the Americans. Launching a full-scale military attack on Thailand did not make much sense. A better alternative was to make use of Jim. He was to be progressively branded as a defector. An ongoing campaign on his demerits was to follow. Given his past background as a spy, the Thai government would eventually be cornered into an embarrassing situation for knowingly closing an eye on his covert activities. Over time, it would be forced into a position where it would have to come up with some sort of a compromise to appease the communists. What the communists were really looking forward to was that Thailand would take the initiative to shut down all the American air bases on its soil. By doing so, the Americans would be deprived of a military outpost just outside the war-torn Indo-China area.

Most pressmen were also suspicious that the Central Intelligence Agency (CIA) was well aware of this ploy. When queried, the CIA chose to downplay the issue. This caused greater suspicion. The press began to speculate that the CIA could have been involved in a series of behind-the-scene negotiations with the communists. This was the prognosis: the CIA pressed for Jim's release in return for favorable concessions. But the communists were not at all keen to let Jim go as they were unhappy with the dispensations that came their way. Hoping for something better, the communists held on to him.

But what did Peter actually mean when he said that Jim had been abducted to another country but "is not being held for ransom"?

The commonly held reasoning was that the communists were frustrated that they could not make use of Jim to fulfill their political cause. If he was portrayed as a defector, very few people would have believed it. The CIA was well aware of this fact. Not to be outdone, the communists came up with another solution – they kept Jim to help develop the

Solved!

silk trade in Cambodia and China. Cambodia did not have an export-orientated silk industry, producing silk for domestic consumption.

China, on the other hand, had been hard hit by the quality silk which was produced by Thailand. This deprived her of foreign exchange. China was in alliance with Cambodia during the Indo-China war. They were both in need of cash to keep their war plans going. Of all the options available, silk seemed to offer the best returns. As far as they were concerned, it made no sense demanding a ransom for the return of Jim; it made more sense engaging him to help revive their flagging industry.

To a limited degree, this theory was seen to be somewhat logical. But there were many others who were not at all convinced. Quite a few, however, preferred to be more diplomatic about their views: they chose instead to classify Peter's theory as 'interesting'. Richard Noone, a Cambridge anthropologist, was one such person. When told of Peter's participation and the assessment he came up with, Richard had this to say: "If what Peter says is true, then it makes the search for Jim all the more interesting".

Come to think of it, he was right.

Chapter Twelve

On Wednesday, April 26, Richard Noone and his two assistants, Rahim bin Kamman and Toh Pawang Angah Sidek, emerged from the forest. In all, they spent a total of thirty-six hours looking for Jim.

"I am fully convinced," Richard told a group of reporters, "that neither Jim nor his body are in the jungle. We went further into the jungle, starting off from where the police field force men had earlier left off. But we could not find any clue which could be of use in leading us to him.

"During our search, we came across a steep cliff. We had to turn back. I don't think it would have been possible for Jim at his age to have scaled that cliff. Furthermore, I don't think he would have gone as far as we went if he did go into the woods."

When told of Peter's visit and his abduction theory, Richard expressed his surprise at the soothsayer's claim that Jim had been kidnapped and was being held captive in a foreign land.

"Telepathy," he said, "is something new to me. If what Peter says is true, then it makes the search for Jim all the more interesting."

To a considerable extent, Richard was right. The insubstantiality of Jim did create a high level of interest. In Bangkok, for instance, the Thai Silk Company continued to observe his evanescence with great concern. Charles U. Sheffield, the acting manager of the company, announced that their earlier reward for the finder of Jim had been doubled from US$12,500 to US$25,000. This incentive helped to generate a greater degree of attention on Jim's mysterious status. And this was not the only reward which was declared at this point in time. In a separate announcement, a group of Jim's friends came up with an entirely different enticement. They made it clear that they were more than will-

Solved!

ing to sacrifice US$10,000 to anyone who was able to provide them with proof of Jim's death. To a large degree, both offers highlighted the fact that those who knew him well were indeed concerned for him. Much the same too could be said of the Malaysian police. In early May, it announced that it had turned to Interpol for help. This was disclosed by Perak's officer-in-charge of criminal investigation, assistant commissioner U. Santokh Singh. He described the request of the police in seeking Interpol's assistance as a "routine matter". He went on to say that the police had not given up on their quest for Jim. "The hunt," he said, "will continue and investigations into his sudden disappearance are still proceeding." He informed the public that there had been no change to the RM10,000 reward for information leading to Jim's whereabouts. He encouraged those who held any clue to Jim's actual circumstances to make a report at any police station. On its part, he added, the police would see to it that whatever leads that came its way would be attended to accordingly.

Chapter Thirteen

The departure of Jim was not only puzzling; it also stirred many to come up with their very own conclusions. One such speculation was that while he was in the forest, Jim accidentally came into contact with an attractive 'love-starved' girl. After a brief acquaintance, he went ahead and married her.

An Iban, when told of this reasoning, found it to be rather hard to accept. He said, "Such a development is unlikely to have happened. What could have possibly unfolded is this: while he was trying to find his way through the jungle, he could have been spotted by an aborigine without his even knowing it. I suppose the native must have made use of his blowpipe and blew a dart straight into him."

A British mind reader, on the other hand, did not think that this was likely the case. He alleged that Jim was very much like an old elephant. Jim, he sensed, was well aware that it was "more or less time for him to die. To die in the city of Bangkok made no sense at all to him. The impenetrable vegetation of the Malaysian 'alps' seemed more appropriate. So on Sunday, March 26, when the Lings were in their bedroom and his friend Constance was in a different room, he quietly left the house and made his way for the woods. While he was on the uncultivated land, he kept on walking for as long as his legs could carry him. A few days later, he collapsed in exhaustion and died."

A Caucasian lady, however, made it out to be otherwise. She mentioned that she was informed by "a very reliable source that Jim was run down by a truck while he was heading for the main road. On realizing that he had done wrong, the driver quickly dumped the mangled body into the rear of his vehicle and later saw to it that it was disposed of quietly."

Solved!

However, a lawyer, when informed about this piece of speculation, took it to be "a little out of this world". Based on reports which he read of in the press, he was sure that Jim did not go into the forest at all. "If he had done so," he said, "he would have been found."

"Jim," he reasoned, "was not a stupid person. He must have been in some difficulty which he found hard to overcome. Such being the case, he had to make it appear as though he was going for a long-deserved vacation. Along the way, he vanished from the scene."

Agreeing with whatever the lawyer had had to say, an ex-serviceman from the Intelligence Unit of the Malaysian Armed Forces adduced that "it is obvious that Jim shrewdly took a side trip without keeping anyone informed. That is why there was no ransom for his release or any information whatsoever with regard to his likely whereabouts."

A one-time correspondent, when quizzed about Jim's vanishment, came up with an entirely different interpretation. He said: "When Jim came to the Highlands, many made it out that he was coming over for a short holiday. But few were aware of the fact that the Highlands was actually the gateway for his long established drug business.

"Yes, Jim was involved in drugs. When he first came to Thailand, he saw the potential for making a vast fortune out of dealing with drugs. He knew that if he had gone directly into the trade, it wouldn't be long before the authorities would come after him. The best way out was to establish a decent business to serve as a front for whatever plans he had for his future dealings in drugs. By doing so, the chances of his being caught would be narrowed down to a considerable extent.

"From the way he conducted and carried himself, many took it that he was solely responsible for being involved with the silk trade. But what they didn't realize is that there was actually more to it than just being connected with silk. Jim was not only synonymous with the silk trade; he was also associated with drugs in a big way. For years he has been suspected as being one of the many drug lords of the Golden Triangle. To the best of my knowledge, he is the only person that I know of who got along well with all the leaders of the warring parties in Indochina. How did he manage it? Simply put, he had both the money and the resources to do just this. Just as much as he needed them, they in return needed him as well. He needed them to police his drug business; on their part, they needed him to see the fulfillment of their political cause."

The late pressman went on to say that Jim's drug set-up was not as complex as what one would make it out to be. According to him, the drugs were periodically brought into the country from across the Thai-Malaysian border. He added, "The boundary line at that time was loosely guarded. This was so for the plain reason that it was far too long and densely forested. Jim cleverly capitalized on this drawback to the best of his ability. He saw to it that the drugs were brought over to the resort via a dirt track which terminates at the township of Ringlet.

"It is a fact that Jim was no stranger to Foster's Lakehouse (now The Lakehouse). It was from here that he oversaw the overall distribution of his drugs.

"I believe there are two reasons as to why he got 'lost'. In the first instance, he could have deceived the members of his syndicate, taking a vast sum of money. The other could be that the long arm of the law was now closing in on him. Of the two, the former seems to be more in line."

That said, how then did Jim manage to depart from the outpost without leaving a single trace behind?

"He discreetly made his way for Ringlet," confided the former correspondent. "It was from here," he observed, "that he took one of the weather-beaten tracks which ensured his exit out of the resort."

While some were comfortable with whatever the ex-journalist had had to say, there were just as many who were not at all in agreement with him. A number of Thais, for instance, were of the conviction that he could have, knowingly or unknowingly, positioned a newly acquired image in an entirely wrong area of his house. This act of carelessness, they sensed, could have brought about much sorrow and anguish to the idol in question. To teach him a good lesson, the spirit made him go round in circles. Being stubborn, he chose not to repent. It was because of this, they reasoned, that he has continued to remain disorientated all this while.

Apart from the Thais, the Malaysians too had their very own views: it ranged from his being "kidnapped" to his "slipping and falling into an animal trap".

Across the Causeway, however, most Singaporeans were of the opinion that Jim could have been lost "as a result of losing his sense of direction". They felt that "if he could get his bearing right, he should be able to find his way back in no time at all".

When asked for his assessment, an ex-Rover scout agreed with this line of thinking. He acknowledged that the Highlands have long been

Solved!

noted for its intricate network of tracks. Paths 4, 9, 11 and 12, he observed, are suitable for family strolls. Paths 3, 5, 7 and 10 involve a much longer walk. As for paths 2 and 8, he was prepared to classify them as "comparatively steep". He added that "although most of the trails are moderately short, there is still the possibility of combining a few paths to make for a more interesting walk. An example would be the combination of paths 2, 3 and 8.

"If Jim had taken this route at 4.30 pm, he would have been back by 7.30pm. It is indeed unfortunate that he did not do so. I am of the impression that he could have left one of the paths along the way. While drifting into the jungle, he could have ended up being disorientated. For a moment, he could have been in a situation where he just did not know what to do. The first option was to backtrack; the second was to continue on from wherever he was. Of the two, I suppose, he must have opted for the latter. This was so because time was no longer on his side. He knew that if he had chosen to make an about turn, he would have in no way been able to make it back before sunset. The best option was for him to carry on from wherever he was. While he was in such a situation, he had to depend on his knowledge of bush lore to see him through whatever difficulties he was in. Sad to say, this did not turn out to be the case."

When asked for his assessment, Dr Ling mentioned that it is a fact that Jim "was by nature an adventurous person. (It is common knowledge) that he had a particular interest in wild plants". He felt that it was more these two factors than anything else that could have "carried him further into the jungle".

Alan Tan, however, saw it differently. The ex-banker was sure that Jim had another motive for going into the jungle.

"Jim," he felt, "was actually hard pressed for cash. He needed the cash not only to pay off his share for the expansion of his company's new building; he also needed it to buy back some of the shares which he had given away. His only asset was his famed 'House on the Klong'. But it was not at all easy for him to get rid of it. If he had done so, it would have been indicative to both his friends and business associates that he was in bad shape.

"The best way out was for him to get a loan. I think this was exactly what he did: he came to the hill camp with Constance so that he could borrow a fixed sum of money from Dr Ling.

"When they arrived at the 'acropolis', the subject of a loan was not at all mentioned. The next day, I suppose it was very much the same. But on Sunday, while they were having a picnic, he took it as a good opportunity to raise the issue. I am quite sure Dr Ling must have been taken aback when the topic was brought up.

"I suspect Dr Ling could have politely turned down his request with the excuse that his money was tied up in some business venture. This could have caught him and the others off-guard. For a moment, several things could have crossed his mind. He must have felt rather small. To cover up for his lost pride, he began to show them the other side of his character. He became easily irritated at whatever that was being discussed at the picnic. To capture their attention, he got up and started collecting the plates. The Lings noticed the sudden change in his character. They knew he was annoyed. To pacify him, they suggested that he take a nap in the open. But he was not in favor of it. In short, he was more for the idea that the picnic be called off. Not to be a further source of annoyance to him, the Lings and Constance complied with his request.

"While they were heading back, he still harbored the hope that Dr Ling would change his mind. He was pretty sure the odds were in his favor. But it didn't turn out to be that way. When the two ladies and Dr Ling retired to their rooms, he chose instead to sit in the hall. He came to realize that he had to go on living with his problems. It was more his pride than anything else that made him think that way. He took it that his problems were 'here to stay and won't be gone tomorrow'. It was nothing but a vicious cycle which involved money and the borrowing of more money. He came to understand that he was now sinking into a bottomless pit. To come out of this sorry situation, he made up his mind to take his own life.

"It did not take him very long to work out a sound plan. The emphasis was on simplicity. The first thing he did was to leave his jacket, pills, a packet of cigarettes and a lighter behind. He then headed for the Lutheran Mission bungalow. He stopped there for a short while to take a look at the garden. Once he was sure he was seen, he left the place. Later, he was seen standing on a plateau for about half an hour. The last person to see him was a hotel employee who saw him take the track (path 4) which leads to the golf course.

"He was now free to do whatever he had earlier planned to do. He knew that the time was now right for him to make a quick exit. He was sure that once this happened, the police would come around and look

Solved!

for him. The people who saw him would keep the police informed of their seeing him. They would all end up pointing to different directions. This would leave the police puzzled as regards his actual whereabouts. Their search would have to be planned in such a way that some areas be given more attention than others. While this was happening, he would have had more than enough time to go into the woods to take his own life. And that was exactly what he did. Best of all, he did it without leaving a single trace behind."

Siva, a popular guide at the hamlet, found Alan's conclusion rather hard to believe. "It's simply ridiculous," he said, "that Jim went into the wilds to commit suicide.

"I have to admit I was rather young when Jim was declared as lost. But as a result of my being a resident of this area for more than three decades, I can safely say that if Jim had gone into the forest to commit suicide, his remains would definitely have been found. There is just no way that one could end up committing suicide out here without leaving some sort of proof behind.

"The jungle out here is unlike any other: for decades, it has been home to thousands of people. These people know the place like the back of their hands. If anyone were to collapse and die in their backyard, they would be the first to know of it. In time to come, the authorities too would be made aware of such an eventuality."

Siva was not alone in his reasoning. Dr Ammundsen, Constance and Dean were also in agreement that Jim did not come over to the Highlands to end his life.

Dr Ammundsen was positive that Jim "was a man (who was) very interested in his work. I don't think there was anything in his mental outlook which would make him do a thing like that."

Constance, on the other hand, was sure that Jim "was looking forward to going back to Bangkok".

"He was a tired man," she said, "that is why he came here for a holiday."

Dean, who was with him the night before he left Bangkok, was affirmative that he saw no signs of depression in him.

"Jim," he observed, "is a very stable individual. It is unlikely of him to have taken his own life."

If Jim did not commit suicide, what then could have possibly happened to him while he was at the terminal? Some of his friends were of the opinion that he could have been kidnapped while he was all by himself. They did highlight the fact that he got to know far too many communists during his lifetime. They were quite sure that the communists with whom he was acquainted were the ones who actually abducted him.

One spin on this theory was that a convoy of five cars was seen going up the resort just before Jim went astray. The same five cars were later seen coming down the road just after he was proclaimed as lost.

Many who were keeping close tabs on his disappearance were now more than prepared to accept the fact that he was actually kidnapped by an organized gang. But there was a funny twist to the described episode: of the thousands who were at 'Cameron's Land', only one person from Tapah remembered seeing a convoy of five cars with Thai license plates plying up and down the haunt. However, one thing is for sure: an investigation by the Malaysian police revealed that such an event never did take place. As such, the sighting of the attendant must be the imagination of one man more than anything else. However, there was a separate development which did not at all go unnoticed: on the day of Jim's sudden fading from view, two black limousines were also spotted at Tapah. A couple of hours later, both vehicles were not at all to be seen.

On the international front, quite a few believed that it was the Chinese government who had had a hand in bringing Jim under their shadow. For a number of years, the Chinese silk industry was hard hit by the quality silk which was being produced by Thailand. The Chinese, however, chose not to publicize it for fear of losing face. To outdo the Thais, the Chinese came up with a plan whereby Jim had to leave Thailand for Malaysia. While he was in Malaysia he was to create the impression that he was there for a short holiday. When it was more or less time for him to leave, the necessary arrangements would then be made for him to fly in to China. Once in China, he was to see to it that their ailing industry was revived. To get him to do just this, it is deemed that the Chinese government arranged a transfer of US$1 million to a foreign bank which was based in Bangkok. Many assumed that Jim withdrew the money prior to his coming over to Malaysia.

Perceived or real, the topic of Jim's vanishing continued to grow with each and every passing day. The speculations that surfaced led many to believe that he could either be in Malaysia or Cambodia. But why not China? The Chinese silk industry was long established before the arrival of Marco Polo. Why then, debunkers argued, should the Chinese be dependent on Jim when they knew the trade inside out?

Solved!

Chapter Fourteen

The last appearance of Jim was unique in many ways: for the next few weeks, his eclipse was not only discussed at length; equally interesting, it became a subject which refused to die off on its own.

While many were still trying to figure out how he got lost, an odd development came to light approximately five months after he went astray. This incident not only threw up a lot of questions; it also added a fresh dimension to his strange exit from the resort.

On Wednesday, August 30, it was reported that his older sister, Mrs. Katherine Thompson Wood, 74, was found dead in her Pennsylvania home. The police were of the opinion that a blunt object was used to carry out the murder. But they were positive that her death had no relationship whatsoever to Jim's departure from the refuge. While some were inclined to accept it as such, there were just as many others who were not at all prepared to do so.

What was it that made them doubtful? To begin with, the police mentioned that the motive for her murder had nothing to do with robbery. Since that be the case, why then was she killed? Furthermore, why did her two dogs remain silent while she was being attacked? Were her dogs afraid of the murderer or was it that they knew the killer?

Whatever it is, the commonly held reasoning was that the assassin was trying to get something out of her. Being unable to do so, she was clobbered to death.

For quite some time, many took it that the CIA had a hand in her assassination. Later, it was also speculated that the communists' involvement too was not at all to be ruled out altogether.

The murder of Jim's sister not only left many in want for an answer; it also added fuel to a new round of speculation. Most of Jim's friends

Solved!

were of the opinion that there was a link between her death and his abscondence from the hideaway. But they found it hard to prove that the two events were, in all probability, connected to one another. Such being the case, they had no choice but to hold on to their observations until further evidence was made available.

Just as the hotly debated speculations were about to die off, an interesting character came into the scene. He was Robert McGowan, an ex-major from the British army. He told a group of Jim's friends that he had seen Jim in a vision. He claimed that Jim was imprisoned in Cambodia and that he could be found in a double-storied residence in the district of Stung Treng. He went on to say that just outside the building was a wooden wheel. The wheel, according to him, was "leaning quite close to the entrance of the house".

At first, Robert was made out to be another quack. It was only after he drove down the streets of Bangkok blindfolded that his words were taken seriously. It was alleged that a group of Jim's friends later got together to organize a rescue mission of their own. To add punch to their operation, they recruited the services of an ex-Gurkha. Their plan was to leave Thailand for Cambodia in a private plane. On nearing Stung Treng, the pilot was to create the impression that the airplane was encountering some mechanical problem. On landing, all were to pay particular attention to the described structure. Once spotted, the Gurkha was to burst into the unit and rescue Jim. He was to ensure that Jim was immediately brought over to the 'stalled' aircraft. After this was done, the plane was to head back for Thailand without any delay.

While their scheme was being hatched, the CIA somehow came to know of it. On the day the party was supposed to leave, a few agency officials met up with them and advised them to do away with their plan. For the next few days, they felt rather dejected that their mission had had to be abandoned. But deep inside them, they were not at all keen to see it end just like that. A few weeks later, a handful of them got together and privately arranged for the Gurkha to cross into Cambodia. He spent a fortnight in Stung Treng. While moving around, he came across a number of two-storied houses – none of them had a wheel leaning against it.

Chapter Fifteen

The casting about for Jim did not end at Stung Treng: it, in fact, marked the extension of more searches in other areas as well. Most of the investigations, if not all, were carried out in earnest. But the various groups that went out of their way to look for him were in no way successful in their effort to find him. A good example was a Japanese team who crossed the Thai border town of Ban Aranyaprathet in early 1968. After spending a week in the rural communities of Siem Pang and Virachei, they came to the conclusion that Jim was not at all to be found in Cambodia.

What was it that made them want to head that way? At one stage, there was a strong rumor in the Thai capital that Jim was being held captive in the northeastern part of Cambodia. Later, it was believed that if he was not being detained in Stung Treng, then, in all probability, he could be at either Siem Pang or Virachei. The Japanese, who were told of the failed attempt at Stung Treng, decided to give the other two municipalities a try. But their hope of coming into contact with him turned out to be nothing but a disappointment.

After this endeavor, there were three other events which helped to bring about a fair measure of excitement into pinning down his likely whereabouts. The first was a report of his being sighted at the Thai beach resort of Ko Samui. Later, it was discovered that the Caucasian who looked like Jim was not him; he was in fact a German who was enjoying a long stay at the popular retreat.

The next development which brought about a degree of interest in the possibility that Jim is still alive was an alleged photograph of him which was featured in a now-defunct tabloid. It depicted him in the company of four Asian-looking men. In the picture, all five were in the

Solved!

process of sharing a meal. They had a bowl (of rice?) in one hand and a pair of chopsticks in the other. The picture generally gave the impression that he was going through much hardship and difficulty. He, like the rest, was portrayed as having to squat to have his meal. Later, it was confirmed that the Caucasian was not Jim – he was actually an American who was captured by the Laotians at the height of the Vietnam War.

The other episode which caught the attention of many involved an Indian mystic by the name of Dadi Balsara. He informed the press that he came to have an interest in Jim's predicament as a result of reading about it in the newspapers. He said that a few days after Jim was reported as lost, he took the trouble to draw out Jim's 'astrological chart' to see if the 'stars' could provide him with a clue as to where Jim could be found. From the chart, it became apparent to him that Jim was alive and that he was abducted for personal reasons.

While he was in Bangkok, he got to know several people who were, in one way or another, close to Jim. In getting to know them, he was not only brought over to Jim's house; just as noteworthy, he was also extended the privilege of lying down on Jim's bed. Whether his senses were alerted to anything or not, he chose not to disclose it in the open. Much later, it became evident that he was really of not much of a help. At the end of it all, he left the scene and nothing more has been heard of from him ever since.

After the unfolding of these events, the hunt for Jim slowly came to a close. Finally, the painful news had to be made known: a Thai court, at the request of some of his family members, went ahead and pronounced him dead. The declaration was made in early 1974, that is, exactly seven years after he went off course.

It could be acknowledged that the decision of the court caught many by surprise. For the next few months his fate was hotly debated in quite a number of places. But the answers that readily surfaced generally led no one anywhere.

Chapter Sixteen

The mystery of Jim was not only a topic which enjoyed a fair measure of flexibility; it was also a subject which many found hard to resist. From the time he went astray, more than a dozen theories have been advanced to best explain his insubstantiality. So far, none have been particularly convincing. Why is that so? Simple.

To begin with, what were Jim's motives for coming over to the Highlands? Moreover, what did he have in mind on completion of his stay at the area? According to Constance, "…he was a tired man… That was why he came here for a holiday." She was also quoted in the press as saying that "he was looking forward to going back to Bangkok", that is, on completion of his outing at the refuge. But was this his real plan? Not so. What Constance was actually trying to put across was that Jim had in fact made plans with her and the Lings to head for Singapore on the morning of March 27. The Lings were to drive him to the city state so that he would be able to keep his dinner appointment with Francis Joseph Galbraith, the US ambassador to Singapore and Edward Pollitz, an American capitalist who was seriously looking into the possibility of establishing a textile outfit in the republic. But a day earlier, he went missing. How did this come about? Could it be that he got involved in a 'planned disappearance' or was it an 'unforeseen circumstance' which unfolded on its own? Based on circumstantial developments, the former seems to be more the case. How come? After leaving the recreation home, he was reportedly seen by five witnesses. Unique as it may seem, none of them was right in their description of him, save the cook from the Lutheran Mission bungalow. She, however, made a small mistake by saying that he had on a pair of gray slacks when in actuality they were of a dark blue shade.

Solved!

As for the rest, it was either they saw the wrong person or the timing of their sightings was not at all correct. Che Fatimah binte Mohamed Yeh, the cook from the mission home, remembered seeing him at about 4pm. The servant employed at the Overseas Mission Fellowship bungalow also noticed him at around the same time. But that is not all. There were two other ladies who also spotted him at about 4pm. One remarked that she observed him at a side road talking to two passers-by. The other stated that she saw him about a stone's throw away with a camera slung over his shoulders.

The only male witness who had a glimpse of him was an employee of the former Eastern Hotel. He was sure he saw someone who resembled Jim heading in the direction of the track which led to the golf course. But his description of him was not as one would expect. As such, his evidence was not at all taken seriously.

Out of the five who supposedly saw him, only one gave an accurate description of him. Based on her testimony, it was clear that Jim left the Ling's domain and made a right turn for the Lutheran commune. The distance between the two addresses is about 1,440 meters. What was it that made him want to head in that direction? The only clue available is that approximately five years ago he was stung by hornets about a kilometer from Moonlight. He did inform Constance and his other friends that he would like to visit this same spot on his next trip. Whether he did so or not, no one really knows. But a few conclusions could be drawn as a result of his being seen at the Lutheran enclave: one, he had to stroll past Sunlight villa which is, incidentally, about 50 meters from where he stayed; two, for the next 480 meters, he had to carry on with his walk in order to reach the precinct's T-junction; three, on reaching the intersection, he had to make a right turn to ensure his ultimate arrival at the mission home; four, while walking along Jalan Kamunting (Kamunting Road), he had to cross two driveways which led to the residences of Nos. A43 and A44; five, after clearing both stretches, he had to carry on with his walk for another 560 meters; finally, after he had done all this, he found himself at the road barrier which vaguely separates the street from the domicile.

While he was standing at the barricade, there were two options open to him: one, he could have gone past the metal work and continued on with his walk; or two, he could have made an about turn and returned to where he first came from. Of the two, he chose the former knowing fully well that he had no right whatsoever to intrude into the grounds of the hermitage. By virtue of the fact that he did so, it is clearly indicative that he was either on the lookout for someone or he was anxious to satisfy his curiosity as to whether there were any occupants residing at the unit. But what caught him by surprise when he got to the building was this: he had expected to see the façade of an imposing chalet; what he saw instead was the rear of a storage area followed by the kitchen.

While he was in the compound, it also became clear that he was not on the lookout for a hornet's nest. The cook who spotted him mentioned that she "… saw him come up the road (in other words, the 230-meter driveway)… He stopped for a while *to take a look at the garden. While looking at the plants*, he did not speak to anyone. A short while later he left the premises…"

What was it that made him want to leave the place? Simple. While he was in the complex, it became obvious to him that he had reached a dead end. Since that was precisely the case, he had no choice but to return to where he first came from.

While walking back, there were three options opened to him: one, he could have scaled the steep slope to his left; two, gone down any one of the ravines to his right; or three, carried on with his walk. Since age was not on his side, it could be taken that he must have continued on with his walk until he was about to reach the road intersection. While approaching this spot, he had the choice of either slowing down or stopping to take a rest. If he had decided to carry on with his walk, he would have not only reached the divider; he would have also had the alternative of making a left turn or a right turn. A left turn would have seen him back at Moonlight; a right turn would have led him on to the main road. Since he failed to return and he was also not at all seen by anyone, then, it could be taken, that he remained on Jalan Kamunting for quite some time.

But could such an assessment be classified as correct? Some may say 'yes' but there may be many others as well who would be more than prepared to say 'no'. But what Richard Noone had had to say not only made sense; it also did highlight the fact that Jim could have chosen to remain on Jalan Kamunting for as long as he had wanted to.

"I am fully convinced," Richard said, "that neither Jim nor his body are in the jungle."

What was it that made him come to such a conclusion? Simply put, Richard, a Cambridge-trained anthropologist, was not only at home with the jungles of the territory; by the same token, he was also held in

Solved!

high esteem by the inhabitants of the woods. There was no denying that he did spend about thirty-six hours in the wilderness looking for Jim. But what was all the more striking was that while he was in the green quietude, he had the rare opportunity and distinction of coming into contact with a few aborigines. As a result of his conversing with them, he could sense that they were in no way trying to hide anything from him. As a matter of fact, when H.D. (Pat) Noone, his elder brother, was declared as lost in the dense forest of Perak in the 1940s, it was the native community who informed him of his brother's fate. It was not a pleasant story for him to hear but Richard had to bitterly accept it the way it was presented to him.

Of all the people who were in one way or another involved with the sleuthing of Jim, it could be confirmed that Richard was the only authority who was bold enough to proclaim that "neither Jim nor his body are in the jungle".

Since Jim did not at all go into the tangled vegetation, where then did he go to? From about 1.45pm to around four, he was on one particular section of Jalan Kamunting. A little after four he was on this same road but, this time around, he was moving in an entirely different direction. What was his purpose for being on this bridle path for more than two hours and on it again for a questionable period of time?

Whatever it is, it surely had nothing to do with his being anxious about the hornets which stung him about five years ago. All told, it certainly had a lot to do with his keeping of an appointment which he had made earlier on. But what indications are there to highlight that this was precisely the case? According to Helen, Jim "appeared nervous (while they were at the picnic) ... and he seemed anxious to get back early." If that be so, then at what time did they all get back to their vacation home? Dr Ling remembered their returning to the cottage at about 2.30pm. He was later quoted in *The Straits Times* as saying that he "... heard footsteps pass by my bedroom door (at) about 3.30pm and (I) presumed it was Mr. Thompson taking a stroll."

Helen, however, had something else to say: she informed the widely circulated *Eastern Sun* that Jim told her and Constance "Good night, sweethearts" at 1.30pm. When asked why the "good night" bit during noon, Helen remarked that "it has always been our practice despite the time of the day or night to say good night whenever we wanted to retire for the night or for a siesta". The report concluded, "with the wave of his hand, he was gone".

Where then did he head for? Since he left the chalet at about 1.30pm, it could be taken that he reached the T-junction of Jalan Kamunting at around 1.45pm. After making a right turn, he spent more than two hours making his way to the Lutheran Mission bungalow. Why did he have to opt for this route when there were so many other avenues available to him? Put in a simple way, he felt comfortable with this particular stretch of road because it was a suitable spot for his final appearance at the resort. In all, there are only three units situated along this 680-meter boulevard. After the Lee villa (unit No. A44), hardly anyone makes use of the rest of the road save those who are on vacation at the Lutheran abode. He was aware that by remaining on this 560-meter stretch of road, the odds of his being chanced upon were as good as zero. Since Helen and Dr Ling were not in agreement with whatever they had had to say, then it could be treated that Jim's "mysterious" disappearance from the old British station was nothing but a conspiracy. Since that be so, then it is not at all necessary to get involved in a guessing game as to who picked him up and where exactly he was dropped off. Come to think of it, all this was planned long before he came over to the Highlands.

Solved!

Postscript

Move over the Lings, Constance and what have you. To date, volumes have been written about Jim Thompson, by far, the best known legend of Southeast Asia. Of the many who wrote about him, none have come quite close to solving his abscondence from the resort. There are two reasons for this: one, it could be that the authors were not at all aware that Jim actually left the Ling's estate at 1.30pm; or two, they chose not to know about it. Of the two, the latter seems to be more the case. As such, his eclipse from the retreat has not only gone on to be an unsolved mystery; it has also led many to go on a wheel spin.

For the last three decades, the mystery of his departure has not only been a topic which has enjoyed a fair measure of ambiguity; just as interesting, it has also been a subject which many a theorist have found hard to put aside.

I first came to have an interest in Jim's disappearance as a result of reading about it in the newspapers. My initial impression was that he got lost as a result of falling into a pit of quicksand. Years later, I came to realize that this was not so.

In 1994, while on a trip to the Highlands, it came as a surprise to me that in spite of the fact that he vanished more than 25 years ago, the memory of his insubstantiality was still fresh in the minds of many. What also caught my attention was this: some of the residents of whom I spoke to were pretty sure that he must have had a hidden motive for coming over to their neighborhood. But, due to a considerable lack of evidence, they had to put away their views.

While I was at the retreat, I somehow came to have an interest in his absconding all over again. To satisfy my curiosity, I took the route which he took just after he had left Moonlight. While walking down

Solved!

Jalan Kamunting, several questions crossed my mind: One, why did he have to choose this route when there were so many other avenues opened to him? Two, was he really on the lookout for a hornet's nest? Three, what was his purpose for heading for the Lutheran Mission bungalow? Four, was he aware that a holiday home existed at the end of the road? Five, while he was at the complex, what made him want to leave the place? Six, on his way back, did he scale the steep slope to his left? Last but not least, did he in any way have an appointment to be picked by someone of whom he had earlier made arrangements with?

After giving it serious thought, it dawned on me that there was really more to it than his being on the lookout for a hornet's nest. On my return from the hill station, I went through a stack of files to see if I could pinpoint the exact time he left the cottage. To the best of my knowledge, I remember being told that he left the mansion at about 1.30pm. What later proved to be a disappointment to me was this: most reports, if not all, mentioned the fact that he left the villa at about 3.30pm. Much later, while I was going through the past issues of the now-defunct *Eastern Sun*, I came across an article which not only brought to light the issue that he left the mansion at 1.30pm; just as noteworthy, it also highlighted the awareness of both Helen and Constance that Jim did indeed leave the premises for a pre-dinner stroll. Armed with this information, I went ahead to write a book entitled: *...SOLVED! The Mysterious Disappearance of Jim Thompson, the Legendary Thai Silk King*. It was printed and published in the United Kingdom in 1996. Of the thousands who read my book, none in particular came around to say that they were "short-changed".

For this edition, I visited the Highlands again in mid-November 2002. While I was at the haven, I took the occasion to meet up with a number of people. One of them was "Thompson" – not the Thompson who went astray but "Thompson", the taxi driver (see Epilogue). According to him, the inconveniences which Jim and Constance had to put up with while they were at Tapah were not pre-arranged as what many had made it out to be. As far as he was concerned, the change of drivers and vehicles was necessary because the relief driver who had earlier fetched them was not feeling well when he got over to Tapah. Further to this, "Thompson" was also sure that it was more of a coincidence than anything else that when Jim and Constance were asked to board his taxi, there were two Chinese passengers in it. He mentioned that it was Constance, rather than Jim, who was very much against the idea of having to share their ride with the other two commuters. After some deliberation, the other two travelers were asked to get off and "Thompson" saw to it that Jim and Constance were driven on their own to Moonlight.

Apart from my meeting with "Thompson", I also took the opportunity to spend a quiet afternoon at the Jalan Kamunting precinct. I particularly enjoyed my stroll from Moonlight to the Lutheran abode: in short, it not only gave me a nice "feel" of the route which Jim took approximately 35 years ago; it also made me more aware as to why he opted for this path. Except for the presence of a government-owned building (Rumah Istirahat Kumpulan Wang Simpanan Perkerja), nothing much has really changed in the area since the time he was pronounced as lost. Throughout my walk, I did not come into contact with anyone. It was much the same when I first traveled this road some eight years ago.

If you are planning a trip to the Highlands, this is the one place you should not miss. Only after you have taken this route would you be in a better position to understand why Jim was on this road for more than two hours and on it again for a questionable period of time.

Solved!

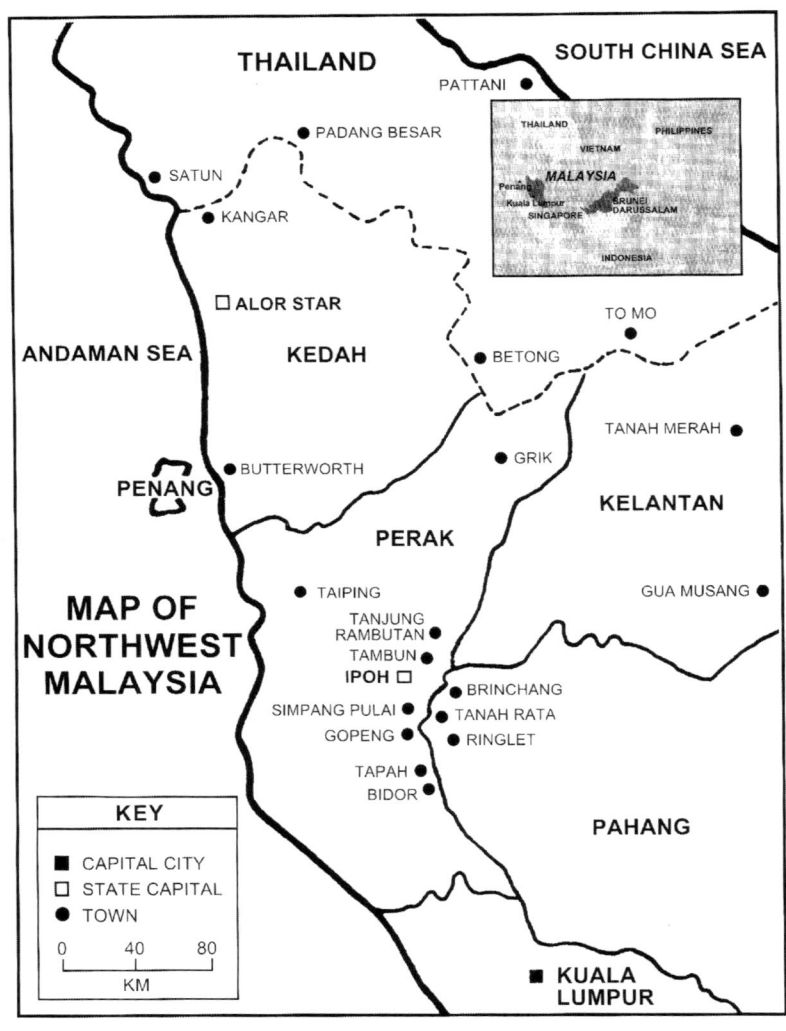

Epilogue

Richard Noone, a Cambridge-trained anthropologist, first came to Malaya (now Malaysia) in 1939. After the death of major P.D.R. Williams-Hunt, the then advisor on aborigines to the Malayan Federal Government, Richard was appointed in 1953 to take over his duties. Richard was the brother of H.D. (Pat) Noone, an anthropologist who was engaged by the State of Perak prior to the Japanese invasion of Malaya. When the Japanese swept down the Malay peninsula in 1941, Richard and his brother were forced to go their separate ways: Pat chose to retire to the woods; Richard, on the other hand, headed for Australia where he served as an Intelligence Officer with the "Z" Experimental Station (ZES) in Cairns, North Queensland. ZES – a unit of the Inter-Allied Services Department – was formed to conduct sporadic raids on the Japanese who were entrenched in Southeast Asia. After the war, Richard continued to work for the Australian Intelligence Service for a short while before moving back to Malaya in 1950 to serve as secretary to the Federal Intelligence Committee. While holding this post, general Sir Gerald Templer, the former British High Commissioner and Director of Operations in Malaya appointed him to head the Department of Aborigines which was later expanded to include all aspects of aboriginal administration throughout the Federation of Malaya. In the course of his work, Richard discovered that one of the peninsula's indigenous clans had a close similarity with the Montagnard tribe that lived in the jungles of Vietnam. In the early 1960s, he led a team of Malayo-Polynesian tribesmen to the Central Highlands to work with them. The two groups had no difficulties getting along well. But the communist government became suspicious of their growing "closeness" and this led to animosity between the

Solved!

Vietnamese and Richard's men. After a while, the ill feelings between the two sides became unbearable and this resulted in Richard and his team leaving the country for good. On his return from Vietnam, Richard took up a posting with the Southeast Asia Treaty Organization (SEATO) as a counter-insurgency advisor. He died of cancer in 1973 in Bangkok, Thailand.

Charles U. Sheffield, who took over Jim as managing director of the Thai Silk Company, died of cancer in 1973. While he was alive, he was steadfast in his view that Jim's disappearance from the Highlands was more the result of an accident than anything else.

Dadi Balsara is at present the managing director of a Singapore-based company which deals in perfumes. He has been in this line of business for more than two decades.

Michael Ian Vermont, an Indonesian of Javanese descent, left Singapore in 1982 for reasons that were best known to himself. It is alleged that prior to his departure, he was involved in a number of "investment schemes" which were more the result of his wild imagination than anything else.

Peter Hurkos passed away peacefully in Los Angeles, California on June 1, 1988. Website *www.stephanyhurkos.com/peter.htm* dated September 9, 2002 had this to say about him:

Peter Hurkos is considered by experts to have been the world's foremost psychic. Born May 21, 1911, in Dordrecht, Holland, he acquired his psychic gift in 1941 after falling from a ladder and suffering a brain injury. He was in a coma for three days at the Zuidwal Hospital. Upon regaining consciousness, he discovered he had developed an ability to pierce the barriers that separate the past, present and future. With stunning accuracy, he was able to see into the unknown.

Hurkos gained worldwide acceptance as a psychic detective, working on cases involving missing planes, persons, and murder victims after his fall. Some of his most illustrious cases were "The Stone of Scone" [London, England], "The Boston Strangler Multiple Murders" [Boston, Massachusetts], "The Missing Thai Silk King, Jim Thompson" [Asia/Thailand], "The Ann Arbor Co-Ed Murders" [Ann Arbor, Michigan], and "The Sharon Tate Murders" [Los Angeles, California].

In 1956, Hurkos was brought to the United States by Andrija Puharich, MD (died 1994) to be tested at his Glen Cove, Maine medical research laboratory. For two-and-a-half years he was tested under tightly controlled conditions. The results convinced Dr. Puharich that Hurkos' psychic abilities were far greater than any he had ever tested (before or thereafter)... a remarkable 90% accuracy.

Edward Roy De Souza

Hurkos' forte was psychometry, the ability to see past-present-future association by touching objects... He had been a consultant to every President of the United States from Eisenhower to Reagan. Hurkos received countless police badges from police chiefs around the world, including one from the International Police Association, and INTERPOL. His Holiness, Pope Pius XII, decorated Hurkos stating: "I hope you will always use your God-given gift for the betterment of mankind. Use it as an instrument to touch the people, to help them."

Pridi Panomyong, the ex-prime minister of Thailand died in France on May 2, 1983. Many who were close to him were positive he had nothing to do with Jim's sudden eclipse from the spa.

Edward Pollitz, the American businessman who was supposed to have a dinner appointment with Jim in Singapore, is the only person to date who has had the rare opportunity of seeing Jim just after his disappearance from the depot. According to him, he was sure he saw Jim leaving a hotel in Tahiti about two months after he was proclaimed as lost. He recalled his attempt of going after him just as he was about to leave the premises. But, before he could do so, Jim quickly got into a waiting car and left the scene.

Seni Pramoj, the former Prime Minister of Thailand passed away on July 6, 1997. He died of a chronic pulmonary disorder at the age of 92. Born into a minor branch of the royal family, Seni studied to be a lawyer and later ended up as the leader of the *Seri Thai* or Free Thai Movement. When the Japanese occupation came to an end, he served as Premier for a short spell in an interim government which was formed in 1946. Thirty years later he made a political comeback and was elected as the country's Premier in 1975 and 1976. He left office in 1975 as a result of an electoral defeat. A year later, his government was toppled in a bloodless coup which was staged by the military.

Constance (Connie) Mangskau – a mixture of both English and Thai by birth – got to know Jim in 1945 when she was engaged as an interpreter for the Allied Services in Bangkok. After the war, she made a career switch and became involved with the retailing of antiques. Jim helped her to open her first shop at the Troadero Hotel. Later, it was he who planned and supervised the construction of her home which was in several ways patterned after his own. With the passage of time, her venture into the sale of antiques proved to be a success. Just before she died in the early 1990s, she was considered by many as being one of Bangkok's leading dealers in the decorative arts and craft of Southeast Asia.

Solved!

George Barrie, Jim's life-long friend and co-founder of the Thai Silk Company, died in Bangkok, Thailand of a heart attack on May 2, 1996. He lived to the age of 94.

"Thompson" – the taxi driver who fetched Jim and Constance from Tapah to Moonlight – has not only mellowed with age; equally intriguing, he has also accepted the nickname "Thompson" despite the fact that he has a given Chinese name. To date, many things have been said about him – some true, some false. For instance, just after it became known that Jim was lost, there has been this talk that Jim hired his taxi and instructed him to stop and wait for him near the T-junction of Jalan Kamunting. This account, sad to say, is not true. According to "Thompson", Jim never made use of his services while he was residing at the chateau. What actually transpired was this: when it became clear that Jim was missing, "Thompson" decided to go into the woods to look for him. While doing so, he got lost along the way. Much later, his family members were informed that his unattended vehicle was spotted near the T-junction of Jalan Kamunting. Sensing that something was not right, they engaged the services of a few aborigines to go out and look for him. A couple of days later, he was discovered in the jungles of Gopeng. After this episode, he became known to one and all in the neighborhood as "Thompson".

Dr Tien Gi Ling was sixty-nine years old when Jim vanished from the old British station. Twenty-five years later, he passed away while he was on a short stay in the United States. His obituary, which was inserted by F.E. Zuellig (Singapore) Pte Ltd, Dr Tan Eng Liang, Hugo Arnet and Pierre Moccand in *The Straits Times* on March 14, 1992, was penned as follows:

Dr T.G. Ling, recipient of the Singapore Science Council's first gold medal, died on March 9, 1992, in Seattle, USA after a brief illness. He was 94.

Dr Ling, a native of Swatow, China, graduated from Shanghai Baptist College (later the University of Shanghai) in 1919 with a degree in chemistry. Two years later he won a competitive scholarship from the American Baptist Mission and went to the USA for post-graduate studies. There he received a master's degree from Brown University in 1922 and a Ph.D. in industrial chemistry from Cornell University in 1924.

In 1926 he returned to China where he developed the first matches that would light during the rainy season in the Yangtze River Valley. Later he was responsible for setting government standards and testing procedures for vegetable oils. For a time he headed the government's inspection and certification laboratory for vegetable oils in Wuhan. There he established a reputation for

Edward Roy De Souza

sincerity and honesty in an area of commerce that had been marked by bribery and corruption.

During World War II he managed the Chinese government's monopoly of materials for making matches. Through his efforts the Chinese match industry became totally self-sufficient, utilizing locally available resources to substitute for imported chemicals which had been cut off by the Japanese occupation.

In 1951 he moved to Singapore where he became affiliated with the Zuellig Company in establishing the first factory (Gold Coin Ltd) for manufacturing scientifically balanced poultry and pig feeds. His introduction of these feeds along with improved breeds and methods of raising poultry and pigs greatly improved the efficiency of producing animal protein in Singapore and elsewhere in Southeast Asia. It also gave rise to a multi-million dollar animal feed industry. The high quality and low price of chicken and pork in Singapore today are the results of his efforts. His contribution was recognized by the Singapore Science Council which awarded him its first gold medal in 1969. The medal was presented by (then) Prime Minister Lee Kuan Yew in a formal ceremony.

Following his success in Singapore and Malaysia, Dr Ling was sought after as a consultant in other countries. He traveled to Indonesia, Thailand, Tonga and Vietnam to give advice on improving their animal feed industries. He was awarded the insignia of the Fifth Class (member) of the Most Noble Order of the Crown of Thailand for his contribution there.

He was formerly the Managing Director of Singapore Agri-Enterprises Pte Ltd, Chairman of the Board of Directors of Island Livestock Pte Ltd, and member of the Boards of Directors of Gold Coin Ltd, National Grain Elevator Ltd and Primary Enterprises Ltd, Singapore. After (his) retirement in 1990 he moved to Seattle.

Dr Ling and his late wife, Helen, were well known socially, particularly in the Singapore American community. She died in 1982. They were featured in the news in 1967 when Jim Thompson, known as the Thai silk king, disappeared from their bungalow in Cameron Highlands, Malaysia. That mystery has never been solved.

He is survived by two brothers, Myron Ling of Mitcham, South Australia and Theodore Ling of Scottsdale, Arizona; one son, Colonel James Ling, US Air Force (retired) of Arlington, Virginia; and three grandchildren.

The Cameron Highlands, which is located in the state of Pahang, is still accessible by road via the towns of Tapah or Simpang Pulai. For non-residents of Southeast Asia it would be better to head for the resort via Kuala Lumpur. The fare for a taxi trip from the airport to the haunt is about RM250 (US$65). The other option is to travel by taxi from the airport to the Pudu Raya bus station. The fare is approximately RM70. From here there are a few bus services which ply directly to the haven. The first service usually starts at around 9am and the one-way fare for

Solved!

the five-hour journey is about RM10.

Moonlight bungalow is still located at No. A47, Jalan Kamunting, 39000, Tanah Rata. Close to the road barrier of the house are several prominent signs viz., "NO ENTRY", "PRIVATE PROPERTY; NO TRESPASSING", "NO LOITERING" and "THIS IS A PRIVATE RESIDENCE NOT A HOLIDAY BUNGALOW NOR FOR LETTING. PLEASE RESPECT OUR PRIVACY". The "BEWARE OF (THE) DOGS" sign, which was once displayed near the letterbox, has since been removed.

The Lutheran Mission bungalow has not changed much since the time Jim trespassed into its property. Tucked at the far end of Jalan Kamunting, it is still a nice place to dwell in especially for those who are on vacation en masse. Contrary to popular belief, the lodge, which is run by the Lutheran Church, is not for the sole purpose of religious retreats; it is actually open to one and all who have chosen the enclave as a place to unwind.

Foster's Lakehouse, a treasure set in the "Valley of Eternal Spring", has undergone a change in name since its gradual conversion from a place of residence to an up-market hotel. Formerly the home of the late colonel Stanley Foster, this landmark, which overlooks the lake, is now known as The Lakehouse. Situated at the 30th Mile of Ringlet, The Lakehouse is approximately nine kilometers from Tanah Rata or about 200 kilometers from Kuala Lumpur, the capital city of Malaysia.

All Souls' Church – the resort's little Church of England – was once known to the early members of its congregation as The Cameron Highlands Church. The history of this establishment can be traced back to well before 1958 when the Vicar of Ipoh and the other members of the expatriate clergy held their services at either the Cameron Highlands Hotel (now the Merlin Hotel) or the Slim School (which is at present the home of the Malaysian Commando Unit). In 1958, the church was extended an offer for a piece of land which used to adjoin the grounds of the former Slim School. The land, which was once owned by Miss Anne L.P. Griffith-Jones, a committee member of the church, was transferred to the Diocese on the understanding that a church would be built on it. For starters, the members of the British army contributed almost a quarter of the church's erection cost of RM4,643 (about US$1,220). Apart from this, they also gave the church a dismantled "Nissen Hut" which has since served as the building's main structure. The church, which is currently situated at Lot 68, Jalan

Pejabat Hutan, 39000, Tanah Rata, was finally completed in September 1958. The name "All Souls' Church" was given during its consecration ceremony on April 30, 1959 by the Right Reverend Bishop H.W. Baines, the then Anglican Bishop of both Singapore and Malaya (now Malaysia). Except for some minor renovation work, the church has remained relatively unchanged up to this day.

The Thai Silk Company, which Jim helped to establish in 1948, continues to grow and flourish up to this day. It is the only silk company which has a control of practically every aspect of its business, that is, from the cultivation of silk worms to the retailing of its finished products. Today, there are more than a hundred shareholders who have a stake in the running of the company. At present, the majority of its shares are being held by the members of the Booth family.

The Raffles Hotel, one of the few 19th century hotels left on this planet, has long been recognized as a jewel in the crown of Singapore's hospitality industry. A stay at any one of its elegant suites is indeed an experience in itself. For quite some time now, there has been this thinking that, of its 103 units, one in particular is distinctively addressed as the "Jim Thompson Suite". This is incorrect. The room which has been mistakenly referred to is the "John Thomson Suite". John, a professional photographer, arrived in Singapore on board the P&O steamer "Emeu" in 1862. Shortly after his arrival, he set up his "Photographic Room" at No. 3 Beach Road, where the hotel's Palm Court wing now stands. He left Singapore in 1865 and returned to England in 1872 after spending some time in China. Fourteen years later, he was called upon to serve as a photography instructor with the Royal Geographic Society. In recognition of his contribution to early photography, the hotel selectively named one of its suites after him.

Jim Thompson's House a.k.a. the 'House on the Klong' is still being considered by many as one of Bangkok's most charming attractions. In any given year, it is not at all unusual for thousands to visit his former home while on leave at the Thai capital. Of late, there has been talk that his museum-like residence may have to be relocated to make way for an expressway that is slated to run through its ground. Before that ever happens, it would be wise to pay a visit to this place while there is still an opportunity to do so.

Solved!

Glossary

Bencharong (ben-cha-wrong): a Thai five-colored chinaware which is noted the world over for its unique form, design and beauty. During the production process, only the finest clay is used to produce the ceramic. The popular combinations of colors are usually that of red, yellow, black, white and green.

Bomoh (bow-more): a Malay word which means medium or witch doctor.

Golden Triangle: a fairly large area in Asia where the common species of poppy (*papaver somniferum*) grows in abundance. This region, which borders four countries, viz., Laos, Burma (Myanmar), Thailand and China has been a hotbed of turmoil and conflict for a number of years. Most of the world's opium, the extract from which heroin is derived, comes from this quarter. Several attempts have been made in the past to discourage the hill tribes from cultivating this crop. But, for the near future, its cultivation is unlikely to be curtailed because the returns derived from this crop are far better than what most other cash crops can offer.

Gunong (goo'-nong): a Malay word for mountain.

Gurkha (ger'-ker/goor'-car): a military race who settled in the province of Gurkha, Nepal around the eighteenth century; a member of one of the famed Gurkha regiments of the British Army.

Iban (e-ban): an East Malaysian aborigine who is more often than not a resident of Sarawak.

Solved!

Jalan (jar-lan): a Malay word meaning road.

Klong (ker-long): a Thai word for canal or waterway.

Kramat hidup (kra-mud he-dope): a medium with supernatural powers.

Southeast Asia Treaty Organization (SEATO): an alliance made up of eight countries, viz., Australia, France, Great Britain, New Zealand, Pakistan, the Philippines, Thailand and the United States which signed the Southeast Asia Collective Defense Treaty in Manila, the Philippines on September 8, 1954. The treaty was spearheaded by the United States after the French were defeated in Indochina. The US felt that an alliance was needed to put a check to the spread of communism in Southeast Asia. Over time, however, the organization did not develop into an effective organization. It failed, in part, because countries such as India, Indonesia and Japan did not join in the grouping. Further to this, its members were usually in disagreement on the actual extent of the communist threat and how it was to be dealt with. Of the eight, only Australia, New Zealand and Thailand were active participants in America's involvement in the Vietnam War (1957-1975). Two years after the war came to an end, the organization ceased to exist.

Spirit house: an outdoor altar where offerings of food and flowers are made to a selected deity. The design of a spirit house is usually quite similar to that of an oriental temple. But there are several factors that have to be taken into consideration before an altar could be classified as consecrated. A fine example would be the selection of an appropriate spot to site the raised structure in relation to its surroundings. If space permits, it is a common practice that it be placed just outside the house. Other than that, it is normal for it be positioned on top of a roof. Of utmost importance, however, is the timing that the spirit takes up residence in the altar. This is customarily left to the judgment of either a Buddhist or Brahmin monk.

Samloh (some-law): a Thai word for pedicab.

Index

A

Aboriginal
    clearing, 28
    community, 27-28, 62
Aborigine
    girl, 47
    settlement, 1, 19, 25, 28, 34
    tribe, 27-28
    witch doctor, 38
Aborigine(s), 2, 15, 20, 33, 38,
    47, 62, 69
Adlai Stevenson, 10
Africa, North. *See* North Africa.
All Soul's Church, 18, 74-75
Allied Services (in Bangkok), 71
Alor Star, 68
Ambassador Hotel, 32
American
    air bases in Thailand, 43
    ambassador, 59
    Baptist Mission, 72
    businessman, 59, 71
    community, 73
    embassy (in Thailand), 5
    prisoner of war, 58
    School, Dalat, 2, 28
    school students, 2, 28
Americans, the, 43
Ammundsen, Dr Einar, 19, 25, 52
Ananda Mahidol, King, 4, 41-42
Andaman Sea, 68
Andrija Puharich, Dr, 70
Aniline, 6
Ann Baxter, 10
Anne L.P. Griffith-Jones, 74
Arlington, Virginia, USA, 73
Arnet, Hugo, 72
Asia-Pacific region, 4
Astrologers, 25
Astrological chart, 58
Australia, 69, 78
Awan bin Osman, 38
Ayutthaya, 9

B

Baines, Bishop H.W., 75
Balsara, Dadi, 58, 70
Ban Aranyaprathet, 57
Bangkok, Thailand, 5, 10, 26, 31-32, 34, 40-41,
    45, 47, 52-53, 56-59, 70-72, 75
Bandits, 39
Bangkrua, 6
Barbara Hutton, 10
Barrie, George, 7, 37, 72
Barry Cross, 20
Batek, 15
Baxter, Ann, 10
Beach Road, 75
Beaton, Cecil, 10
Bebe, 39
Bencharong, five-colored, 10, 77
Betong, 68
Bidor, 34, 68
Bishop H.W. Baines, 75
Black, brigadier general Edwin,
    3, 20, 29, 31-34, 38
Blowpipe, 15, 47
Bomoh (witch doctor), 38, 77
Booth family, 75
Brahmin monk, 78
Brinchang, 14, 17, 22, 26, 68
British
    army, 28, 56, 74, 77.
    army major, 2, 19
    High Commissioner, 69
    mind reader, 47
    servicemen, 2, 28
    surveyor, 13
British, the, 14
Brown University, 72
Brunei, 68
Buddhist monk, 40, 78
Burma (Myanmar), 5, 77
Burmese statues, 10
Butterworth, West Malaysia, 68

C

Cairns, Australia, 69
California, USA, 7, 70
Cambodia, 40, 42-44, 53, 56-57
Cambodian stone figures, 10
Camera, 60
Cameron Highlands, 1-2, 13-15,
    17-22, 32, 39-40, 47-50, 52-53, 55-56, 59,
    61, 63, 65-67, 70-74
Cameron Highlands
    Church, 74
    Hotel, 74
Cameron, William, 13
Camerons. *See* Cameron
    Highlands.
Canal *(klong)*, 5, 78
Capote, Truman, 10
Catholic faith, 28
Caucasian, 47, 57-58
Cecil Beaton, 10
Central Highlands, 69
Central Intelligence Agency
    (CIA), 3, 43, 55-56

Ceylon (now Sri Lanka), 4, 42
Chan, Raymond, 27
Chandeliers, Victorian, 10
Chapel, Protestant, 18, 74-75
Charles Sheffield, 26, 37, 45, 70
Chase, Edna Woolman, 6,
Che Fatimah binte Mohamed
  Yeh, 21, 59-61
Chewong, 15
Chin Peng, 43
China, 44, 53, 72, 75, 77
Chinaware, 77
China-Burma-India war zone, 4
Chinese
  government, 53, 73
  name, 72
  passengers, 33, 66-67
  porcelain, 10
  silk industry, 53
  silk shop, 7
Chinese, the, 53
Chloroform, 39, 42-43
Cholera (inoculation), 32
Chopsticks, 58
Christian (Roman Catholic), 40
Chrysanthemums, 14
Church, 18, 74-75
Church of England, 74
Clairvoyant, 31
Club, golf. *See* Golf club.
Cook. *See* Che Fatimah binte
  Mohamed Yeh.
Communism, 78
Communist, 78
  government, 69
  Party of Malaya, 43
Communists, 39, 43, 53, 55
Constance Mangskau. *See*
  Mangskau, Constance.
Cornell University, 72
Correspondent (ex-). *See*
  Pressman, the late.
Coup d'etat, 40-41
Cross, Barry, 20

D

Dadi Balsara, 58, 70
Dahlias, 14
Dalat American School, 2, 28
Dean Frasche, 29, 31-34, 52
Delaware, USA, 3, 5
Delaware National Guard, 3
Dennis Horgan, lieutenant. *See*
  Horgan, lieutenant Dennis.
Diocese, 74

Dog(s), 22
Dordrecht, Holland, 70
Dowser, 31
Drug
  lords, 48
  trade, 48
Dutchman, 19

E

East
  Asia, 4
  Coast, 3
Eastern Hotel, 21, 60
Eastern & Oriental Hotel, 32
Eastern Sun, 62, 66
Edward Pollitz, 59, 71
Eisenhower, President Dwight,
  71
Embassy, US, 5
"Emeu", 75
England, 75
Entrepreneurs, 10
Ethel Merman, 10
Europe, 4, 7
Extrasensory powers, 38

F

F.E. Zuellig (Singapore) Pte
  Ltd, 72
Farb, Stephany, 38
Federal
  Government, 69
  Intelligence Committee, 69
Federation of Malaya, 69
Firecrackers, 35
Ford II, Henry, 10
Fort Monroe, Virginia, USA, 3
Fortune-tellers, 25
Foster, colonel Stanley, 74
Foster's Lakehouse, 49, 74
France, 71, 78
Francis Joseph Galbraith, 59
Frasche, Dean, 29, 31-34, 52
Free Thai Movement, 4, 41, 71
French, the, 78
French resistance forces, 4
Fulbright, William, 10

G

Galbraith, Francis Joseph, 59
George Barrie, 7, 37, 72
Georgetown, Penang, 32
Gerald Templer, general Sir, 69

German, 57
Germans, the, 4
Glass, Belgian, 10
Glen Cove, N.Y., USA, 70
God,
    faith in, 28
    gift from, 40
Gold Coin Ltd, 73
Golden Triangle, 48, 77
Golf
    club, 1, 17-19
    course, 2, 21, 42, 51, 60
Gopeng, 68, 72
Great Britain, 78
Greece, Prince Michael of, 10
Greenville, Delaware, USA, 3
Griffith-Jones, Anne L.P., 74
Grik, 68
Gua Musang, 68
Gunong Brinchang, 18
Gurkha, 56, 77

H

Hanoi, Vietnam, 43
Helicopter(s), 2, 20, 27, 34
Henry Ford II, 10
Hepburn, Katherine, 10
Heroin, 77
Himalayas, 25
Hiroshima, 4
Holland, 70
Horgan, lieutenant Dennis, 31-34, 38
Hornets, 19, 60-62, 66
House on the Klong, 9-10, 50, 58, 75
Hugh Low, Sir, 13
Hugo Arnet, 72
Hurkos,
    Peter, 38-40, 42, 44-45, 70-71
    Stephany, 38-40
Hutton, Barbara, 10

I

Iban, 47, 77
Idol, 49
India, 14, 78
Indian
    mystic, 58
    restaurant, 32
Indo-China, 43-44, 48, 78
Indonesia, 73, 68, 78
Indonesian, 70
Inspector
    general of police, 26
    Tan Ai Bee, 34
Intelligence
    officer, 69
    unit, (ex-serviceman), 48
Interpol, viii, 46, 71
Interpreter, 71
Intersection, road, 60-63, 72
Ipoh, 22, 27, 33, 58
Irene Shareff, 7
Island Livestock Pte Ltd, 73

J

Jah Hut, 15
Jakun, 15
Jalan, 78
    Besar, 17-18, 61
    Kamunting, 17-18, 60-63, 66-67, 72, 74
    Pejabat Hutar, 74
Japan, 7, 78
Japanese
    High Command, 5
    invasion, 69
    Occupation, the, 41, 71, 73
    occupiers, 4
Japanese, the, 4, 42, 57, 69
Javanese, 70
Jehai, 15
Jengjeng, 15
Jim Thompson. *See* Thompson, Jim.
Jim Thompson Suite, 75
Jim Thompson's House. *See* House on the Klong.
John Thompson Suite, 75
Johnson, Lyndon, 10

K

Kamunting
    Road, 60-63, 66
    precinct, 67
Kangar, 68
Katherine
    Hepburn, 10
    Thompson Wood, 55-56
Kedah, West Malaysia, 68
Kelantan, 14, 33, 68
Kennedy, Robert, 10
Kensiu, 15
Kentaq Bong, 15
Keo, Buddhist monk, 40
Khan, assistant commissioner of police Yusoff, 22-23

Klong (canal), 5, 78
Klong Maha Nog, 10
Ko Samui, 57
Kramat hidup, 33, 78
Kuala Lumpur, 34, 68, 73-74

L

Lake, 22, 74
Lakehouse, The, 49, 74
Lanoh, 15
Laos, 5, 77
Laotians, 58
Lee Kuan Yew, (then) Prime
 Minister of Singapore, 73
Lee Villa, 63
Lieutenant Dennis Horgan. *See*
 Horgan, lieutenant Dennis.
Ling,
 Helen, 15, 17-19, 28-31, 34,
  51, 62-63, 66, 73
 James, 73
 Myron, 73
 Theodore, 73
 Tien Gi, Dr., 15, 17-19, 28-29
  50-51, 63, 72-73
Lings, the, 17-19, 29-30, 32, 47,
 51, 59-60, 65
Looms, 6-8
Los Angeles, California, 70
Low, Sir Hugh, 13
Luang Pibulsongram (Pibul),
 captain. *See* Pibulsongram
 (Pibul), captain Luang.
Lutheran
 Church, 74
 Mission bungalow, 21, 51,
  59-61, 63, 66-67, 74
Lyndon Johnson, 10

M

Mabetisek, 15
Mahidol, King Ananda, 4, 41-42
Malay
 peninsula, 69
 word, 77-78
Malaya (now Malaysia), 69, 75
Malayan Department of
 Aborigines, 38, 69
Malayo-Polynesian tribesmen, 69
Malays, the, 15
Malaysia, 13-15, 26, 42, 53, 68, 73-75
Malaysian
 Air Force, Royal, 27, 34
 capital. *See* Kuala Lumpur.
 commando unit, 74

state, 43
Manila, The Philippines, 78
Mangskau, Constance (Connie),
 13, 17-20, 25-26, 28, 31-34,
 47, 50-52, 59-60, 62, 66-67,
 71-72
Marco Polo, 53
Maugham, Somerset, 10
McGowan, Robert, 56
Media. *See* Press, the.
Medium(s), 26, 28, 34-35, 77-78
Medrique, 15
Merlin Hotel, 74
Merman, Ethel, 10
Michael Ian Vermont, 29-30, 70
Military
 attack, 43
 attire, 40
 representatives, 40
 vehicle, 39, 43
Ming pieces, 10
Mitcham, South Australia, 73
Mintil, 15
Moccand, Pierre, 72
Monk,
 Brahmin, 78
 Buddhist, 40, 78
Montagnard tribe, 69
Moonlight bungalow, 1-2, 17-
 20, 27-28, 31, 33-35, 38-39,
 42, 47, 51, 59-63, 65-67, 72-74
Mountain peaks, 14
Mos, 15
Mustada bin Yahaya, 33
Myanmar (Burma), 5, 77
Mystic, 31, 35, 40, 58

N

Nagasaki, 4
Nathan, superintendent A.S.,
 21, 23
National Grain Elevator Ltd, 73
Native(s). *See* Aborigine(s).
Nepal, 77
New Garden Inn, 21, 60
New York, USA, 6
New Zealand, 78
"Nissan Hut", 74
Noone,
 H.D. (Pat), 62, 69
 Richard, 38, 44-45, 61-62, 69
North
 Africa, 4
 Queensland, Australia, 69
Novelists, 10

O

Office of Strategic Services, 3
Opium, 77
Orang
    Asli, 15, 20
    Kanaq, 15
    Selitar, 15
Oriental Hotel, the, 5, 32
Overseas Mission Fellowship
    (OMF) bungalow, 21, 60

P

Padang Besar, 68
Pahang, 13-14, 33, 68, 73
Pakistan, 78
Palm Court wing, 75
Panomyong, Pridi, 4, 40-42, 71
Papaver somniferum, 77
Patricia (Pat) Thraves, 3, 6
Pattani, 68
Pedicab *(samloh)*, 5, 78
Penang, West Malaysia, 32, 68
Pennsylvania, USA, 55
People's Party, Thai, 40
Perak, 13-14, 34, 37, 46, 62, 68
Perfumes, 70
Peter Hurkos. *See* Hurkos,
    Peter.
"Photographic Room", 75
Pibul. *See* Pibulsongram
    (Pibul), captain Luang.
Pibulsongram (Pibul), captain
    Luang, 41-42
Pierre Moccand, 72
Pius XII, Pope, 71
Plateau, 21, 51
Police, 1-2, 17, 19-23, 26-28, 33-34, 37-38, 46, 51-53, 55
Police field force, 2, 20-23, 27-28, 33, 37-38, 45
Politicians, 10
Pollitz, Edward, 59, 71
Polo, Marco, 53
Pope Pius XII, 71
Poppy, 77
Prajadhipok, King, 40-41
Pramoj, Seni, 4, 42, 71
Prebe, 39
Prebi, 39-40
Press, the, 22, 34, 38, 42-43, 45, 48, 58-59
Pressman, the late, 48-49
Pridi. *See* Panomyong, Pridi.
Pridi Panomyong. *See*
    Panomyong, Pridi.

Primary Enterprises Ltd, 73
Prince Michael of Greece, 10
Princeton University, 3
Psychic, 70
Psychometry, 71
Pudu Raya bus station, 73
Puharich, Andrija, Dr., 70

R

Rahim bin Kamman, 45
Raffles Hotel, 75
Rama
    I Road, 10
    V, King, 10
Rangoon (Yangon), 31
Raymond Chan, 27
Reagan, President Ronald, 71
Resort. *See* Cameron
    Highlands.
Ridge, 21-22
Ringlet, 14, 49, 68
Road barrier, 60, 74
Robert Kennedy, 10
Robert McGowan, 55
Robinson waterfall, 2
Roger's and Hammerstein
    musical, 7
Roman Catholic, 28, 40
Roses, 14
Royal Geographic Society, 75

S

Sabum, 15
Samloh (pedicab), 5, 78
Santa Monica, California, 7
Sarawak, East Malaysia, 38, 77
Satun, 68
School for the Blind, 11
Scottsdale, Arizona, USA, 73
Scout, ex-Rover, 49-50
Seattle, USA, 72-73
Second World War, 3-4, 73
Semai, 15
Semaq Beri, 15
Semelai, 15
Semnam, 15
Seni Pramoj. *See* Pramoj, Seni.
Seremban, 20
Servant, 21, 60
Seri Thai, 4, 41, 71
Shanghai Baptist College, 72
Shareff, Irene, 7
Shee Voon Chin, 27
Sheffield, Charles, 26, 37, 45, 70
Siem Pang, 57

Silk, 6-8, 13, 37, 44, 48
Simpang Pulai, 68, 73
Singapore, 28-29, 34, 59, 68, 70-71, 73, 75
Singapore
    Agri-Enterprises Pte Ltd, 73
    Science Council, 72-73
Singaporean(s), 30, 49
Singh,
    assistant commissioner of police U. Santokh, 46
    assistant superintendent of police Sarain, 28
Siva, the tour guide, 52
Slim School, 74
Smokehouse Inn, 19
Soi Kasemsong II, 10
Somerset Maugham, 10
Soothsayer(s), 28, 31, 34-35, 45
South China Sea, 68
Southeast Asia, 65, 69, 71, 73, 78
Spirit house, 10, 78
Spirit(s), 27, 78
Sri Lanka. *See* Ceylon.
St Paul's boarding school, 3
Stanley Foster, colonel, 74
Station, radio and television, 14
Steamer, P&O, 75
Stevenson, Adlai, 10
Straits of Malacca, 14
Stung Treng, 56-57
Sunlight bungalow, 60
Supernatural, 38
Swatow, China, 72
Switzerland, 41

T

T-junction, 60-63, 72
Tahiti, 71
Taiping, 68
Tambun, 33, 68
Tan, Alan, 50-52
Tan Ai Bee, inspector, 34
Tan Eng Liang, Dr., 72
Tanah Merah, 68
Tanah Rata, 2, 14, 17-18, 22, 26, 31, 33-34, 38, 68, 74-75
Tanjung Rambutan, 33, 68
Tapah, 13-14, 29, 32, 53, 66, 68, 72-73
Tea, 14, 18
Telepathy, 45
Temiar, 15
Temoq, 15
Temple, 27, 78
Templer, general Sir Gerald, 69

Temuan, 15
Tennasserim range, 31
Tennessee Williams, 10
Thai
    baht, 40
    capital. *See* Bangkok.
    car license plates, 53
    court, 58
    government, 43
    houses, traditional, 9
    mystic, 40
    National Museum, 8
    National Stadium, 10
    press, 11
    silk. *See* Silk.
    Silk Company, 7-8, 26, 37, 45, 70, 72, 75
    silk industry, 6-8, 13
    Silk King, The, 11, 73
    Silk Millionaire, The, 11
    spirit house, 10, 78
    stone images, 10
Thai-Malaysian border, 49
Thailand, 4-9, 25, 31, 40-44, 53, 56, 68, 70-73, 75, 77-78
Thais, the, 5, 49, 53, 77-78
The Philippines, 68, 78
The King and I, 7
The Straits Times, 62, 72
Thompson, Jim, 1-11, 13, 15, 17-23, 25-29, 31-35, 37-40, 42-53, 55-63, 65-67, 70-75
"Thompson", the taxi driver, 66-67, 72
Thong Weng, 26-27
Thraves, Patricia (Pat), 3, 6
Tien Gi Ling. *See* Ling, Tien Gi.
Tiger, 22
To Mo, 68
Toh Pawang Angah Sidek, 45
Tonga, 15, 73
Ton-kee (medium), 26
Tower, aerial, 33
Track(s)/Trail(s)/Path(s), ix, 14, 21, 49, 50, 60
Troadero Hotel, 71
Truman Capote, 10
Tulips, 14

U

United States of America, 3, 34, 38, 42, 70, 72, 78
University of
    Pennsylvania, 3
    Shanghai, 72

V

Valentina, 6
"Valley of Eternal Spring", 74
Vermont, Michael Ian, 29-30, 70
Vicar of Ipoh, 74
Vietnam, 43, 68-70, 73
Vietnam War, 40, 58, 78
Vietnamese, 70
Virachei, 57
Virginia, USA, 3
Vogue, 6
Voon Chin, Shee, 27

W

Wah Swee, Yip, 34-35
Washington, USA, 3
Waterfall(s), 14
Waterway, 5, 78
West Point, 3
William Fulbright, 10
Williams, Tennessee, 10
Williams-Hunt, major P.D.R., 69
Witch doctor, 38, 77
Wood, Katherine Thompson, 55-56
Wuhan, China, 72

Y

Yahaya bin Ahmad Hashim, 33
Yangtze River Valley, 72
Yip Wah Swee, 34-35

Z

"Z" Experimental Station, 69
Zuellig Company, 73
Zuidwal hospital, 70